Major Jack Union is the son of an unknown hero of Kabul and a London brothel madam, Belle Union. Jack earned his first military stripes fighting with the Royal Horse Artillery on Mars. His background stopped a public rise through the ranks but as a political (or spy) he found freedom and achieved the rank of Major. This position allowed him the scope to protect the British Empire from Monsters, without too many questions raised. Jack lives in apartments attached to his mother's Regents Park business with his batman, Kent.

How To Bag A Jabberwock

A Practical Guide To Monster Hunting

BY

MAJOR JACK UNION

BOOK GUILD PUBLISHING
SUSSEX, ENGLAND

To
Joanne, Amber and Connor

First published in Great Britain in 2012 by
The Book Guild Ltd
Pavilion View
19 New Road
Brighton, BN1 1UF

Printed and bound in Great Britain by
CPI Group (UK) Ltd, Croydon, CR0 4YY

A catalogue record for this book is available from
The British Library.

ISBN 978 1 84624 753 8

Contents

Foreword

T he fact you are holding this book in your hand means you are either curious, scared or sceptical.

I shall address all those responses in time but, first, allow me to tell you the foundation on which this publication is based and about the lifetime's work that has contributed to its construction.

I am Major Jack Union, a retired operative for the Crown. I have served in many different countries but always under the title of Political. This is a term that is now somewhat losing its old meaning and being replaced by 'intelligence agent' or, more popularly, 'spy'.

Although this title may have been a sufficiently good description of my original role, my country had other plans for my explorations, for it was to be my vocation to rid the Empire of Monsters.

The interesting thing for you at this point is to note your own reaction. If you laughed or baulked at the word 'Monster', then you should read this book purely as an entertainment.

If, however, your reaction was one of horror at having been kept so long in the dark, then I can only apologize for the charade you have been submitted to. I would like to assure you that it is my firm opinion that a pretence which seems necessary for the public good at the time often appears cold and short-sighted with the passing of history. For you, I hope this book throws light on past failings.

For those of you who thought 'At last, a guide!' I can only say 'Welcome!' Be assured: knowledge is power.

For the rest I can only assume you have asked yourself the question ...

What is a Monster?

A Monster is a threat to the Empire. Such threats can take many forms but should not be confused with mere beasts.

I have come across many such monstrous beasts, and my field guides to big game and dinosaur hunting can be read by all those who feel this is more in their line of enquiry.

Monsters should also not be confused with the monstrous acts of Man. My family motto is 'Nothing human is alien to me' — a set of very wise words that keeps me grounded. All men are capable of monstrous deeds and therefore to class men as Monsters would be to blacken myself also.

In this volume you will find everything you need to recognize and identify Monsters, discussion of why they are a threat and thus how to deal with that threat in the most direct way, and with least risk to yourself. Nonetheless, naturally enough you may ask yourself ...

Why is this book necessary?

In 1902 our new King ruled that Monsters had been his mother's, our gracious former Queen's, obsession. The prohibitive costs of maintaining my unit and the supposed lack of evidence for our quarry's very existence were enough to lose us our Government's support. Therefore it is now down to individuals alone to look for the signs and know how to act when confronted with these creatures.

This book is their manual.

Air Kraken

Mankind is taking to the skies in greater and greater numbers. We are travelling in hot-air balloons and also on the impressive airships that are emerging from Europe, not to mention the recent breakthroughs in powered flight.

You may be surprised to find the skies are not a new domain to the Empire and that we have been in them for longer than you may be aware. Keeping them clean, however, has been a struggle and systematic hunting has been going on for many years. Above the clouds is a whole ecological system, with only one predator – the Air Kraken. This system has now been virtually eradicated but Air Krakens still inhabit certain areas and are as much a threat as the other creatures are a wonder.

Description
Huge in size – measuring close on one hundred feet in length – the Air Kraken is made of a purplish, gluttonous substance of remarkable lightness. Their bodies are far from solid and a fairly light pressure can push a solid object right into them. Their shape is flat, like a cuttlefish, with a domed back, surmounted by three gas-filled blisters of immense size. The whole creature is held aloft by these great natural balloons and the body undulates and writhes at all times, sending wave-like ripples along its length.

The Kraken has two vast, flat, dark eyes on either side of its body. They appear lifeless at all times and the lack of a pupil suggests they look all ways at once. Set between these two lifeless orbs is the only non-jelly-like part of the beast – its purewhite ceramic-like beak, cruel and hooked.

Along the underside of the Kraken are numerous tentacles; these are folded back from either side of the beak and pass along the entire length of the belly, streaming out behind. Two fluke-ended tentacles, thicker than the rest, are constantly flung before it with lightning quickness. This propels the creature forward, allowing for amazing turns of speed and aerial manoeuvres

The Krakens often hunt in packs and will attack and devour any living thing in their domain. The more aggressive a Kraken becomes, the darker its coloration. They also become darker after feeding.

This monster will try to circle beneath any prey, slowly pushing them higher into the atmosphere, ensnaring their quarry in the writhing forest of tentacles that they launch forward from beneath their bellies. The Krakens use these moist and greasy tentacles to smother and strangle their food. For more solid prey, such as humans, it is often fairly easy to tear these tentacles asunder. However, if some poor unfortunate were to become completely ensnared, then he would certainly be lost.

Kraken chiefly feed on air whales and giant, incandescent jellyfish. They spawn mid-air, giving birth to live young in their hundreds. These quickly become food for practically every other beast in the air, including adult Kraken.

The young Kraken are more solid than the adults and show many strange variations in markings within a single brood. Perhaps it is those with the best camouflage that survive the feeding frenzy that follows upon their birth. An esteemed colleague of mine has made a collection of some of the Krakens' hides and, if you have the opportunity, I recommend looking up Mr. Peter Harrow, esquire for his collection of young Kraken.

Habitat

The hunting grounds where you can encounter these beasts are shrinking, but that, after all, is the point of a sustained cull. At

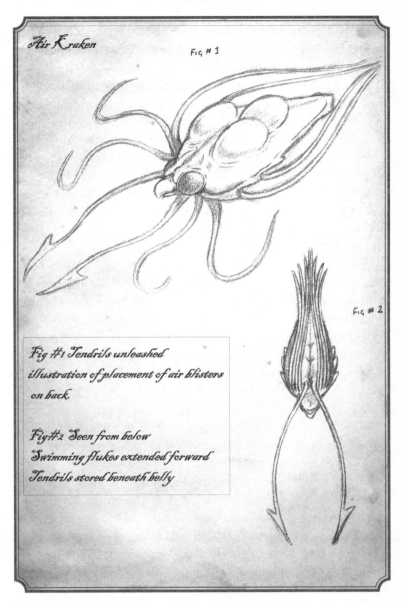

Air Kraken

Fig # 1

Fig # 2

Fig #1 Tendrils unleashed
illustration of placement of air blisters
on back.

Fig #2 Seen from below
Swimming flukes extended forward
Tendrils stored beneath belly

my last reckoning, however, most of the skies above south-west England were still full and some may still be seen in isolated pockets above France and Germany.

Threat

Aerial technology can be only suppressed for a short while, and when the general public gets into the air, the last thing they are going to want to find are 100-foot-long air sharks.

Hunting

Air Kraken are drawn to heat, even a very moderate warmth, and will attack a balloon long before it attacks its crew. This may sound preferable but a punctured balloon will soon lose its hot air and plummet. Therefore using a gas that is lighter than air is a better option than hot air for your ascension.

You will also be ascending to heights where oxygen becomes scarce, so oxygen bags are a necessity.

The matter of weapons, however, is where it gets fun. You get to use a blunderbuss! In all my years of hunting I had never managed to find a use for this highly inaccurate, yet devastating weapon. I owned one, purely for decorative purposes, and when I was told about my first Air Kraken hunt I took it off the mantelpiece and brushed it down. Finally I knew it had a use. If you are not lucky enough to own a blunderbuss in working order, then a wide-bore shotgun will have the same effect. Not as fun, but possibly more reliable.

You need to get to about 30,000 feet or above. Don't go too high or the Air Kraken will get below you and start to circle.

Once you have a Kraken in sight you need to burst its air blisters and bring it down into heavier air – the changed pressure alone will compress and destroy it.

Carry a sharp knife at all times or preferably a sabre. The very moment you feel yourself start to be wrapped in tendrils, start cutting yourself free. Don't try and shoot again – even if you are lucky enough to hit, you will be pulled to your doom along with the Kraken.

It's a distinct possibility that the Air Kraken may catch fire or even explode with so much hot lead flying about. Guns must not be used if the Kraken gets in close to the balloon. In close combat, we take a lead from our Cornish friends and turn to the whaling

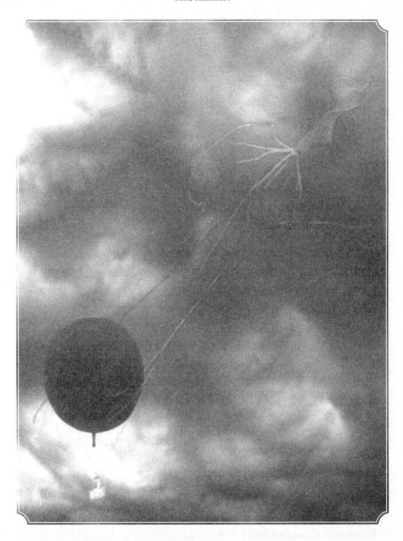

harpoon, a tethered spear that easily passes through the Kraken's lightweight frame and pierces the air sacks with ease.

Personal Account

I must confess that I am not going to enjoy our skies being full of air traffic; people, it seems, are always trying to get somewhere faster and inventing new means to do so. I blame Mr. Fogg myself,

TIPS

You will always need at least four men to a
balloon, one for every side of the basket.

Look as far afield as you can and use
telescopes — the Kraken are at times
almost transparent so you may not spot
them until they are right on top of you.

The upper air is cold and wet
so dress appropriately.

Do practise going up in a balloon to various
heights before you ascend to hunt Krakens.
The extreme altitude can bring on sickness that will render you ineffective.

though, having said that, I am a keen balloonist and enjoy nothing
more than travelling up past the clouds.

On this particular day I was going up in a full balloon. Six men
brave and true. Kent as always was by my side but this time we had
four others with us also — Masters Connor, Doyle, Pagent and
Raymond, all skilled gunmen and all with a fair few ballooning
hours under their belts.

We ascended slowly over the next few hours, an elongated
balloon full of lighter than air gases. The basket was loaded with
oxygen bags, four whaling harpoons, a hamper of food and more
sandbags than seemed healthy. The number of sandbags were
slowly dwindling, which was a shame for Kent, as he had made a
nice seat out of them. We amused ourselves with telling each other
stories and Doyle was definitely turning out to be a good spinner
of tales.

Eventually the balloon was in the upper reaches and we had to turn to our oxygen bags and conversation stopped. The wind replaced the silence with eerie whistling and everybody focused on their telescopes; an array of shotguns and my blunderbuss were primed and ready.

Pagent was the first to see them. Three Kraken were moving down towards us, trying to get themselves beneath our basket. Connor fired first. Although the distance had seemed great, he struck true and the Kraken slumped at an alarming angle; even at a distance, we could see its fluke tentacles splaying about wildly, becoming entangled in the tentacles of one of its companion Krakens.

In the confusion we now all opened fire on the Krakens and the shotguns made light work of the two entangled creatures; unfortunately, however, my blunderbuss did not make the range. I just looked through the telescope, saw the bodies falling into the clouds below and kept my focus fixed on the third and final Kraken, as it found room to circle below us.

I took my chance and opened fire with the ancient weapon; I missed the air sack but instead took off one of its flukes. It changed tack and rose towards us, prompting Raymond to point his shotgun in its direction. Quick as lightning, Doyle grabbed the shotgun's barrel and raised it up, so the round fortunately missed the Kraken — we were all aware (or at least should have been aware) of the danger of a hit this close to us and applauded his prompt action.

Seconds later the balloon lurched as a lifeless eye engulfed our view. I let fly with a harpoon, as did Kent, and the spears passed swiftly through the belly of the beast and out of its back, taking an airsack with them. Tendrils snaked into the basket and we worked our blades quickly to make sure we did not become ensnared.

Connor and Pagent let fly with two more harpoons, two more blisters were lanced and then suddenly the Kraken plummeted ... and our balloon with it!

At first confusion reigned, as we all struggled to retrieve our harpoons by their tethers, thinking that we were somehow snagged. But we continued to descend rapidly, keeping pace with the falling Kraken. It was strange to see how the beast was crushed by the heavy air and soon it dripped like a greasy rain.

We were still falling and a glance upwards showed our balloon was holed ... We were losing precious air, possibly from Raymond's misguided shot. We checked our positioning and the moment we realized we were over the sea we started to ditch our cargo — hampers, air bags, empty sand bags, harpoons and precious guns ... anything we could lay our hands on.

We braced ourselves for the impact but then Doyle had an idea. He slashed the bottom of the balloon wide open and air poured in through the gaping hole, forcing the lighter-than-air mixture upwards into the top part of the undamaged canopy.

We slowed almost instantly, though we were still on our way down and at some speed. We hit the sea at a spine-jarring velocity, but we all cheered together.

The eventual rescue boat found six men grinning like drunken sailors, singing sea shanties at the top of our voices.

Bandersnatch

T he threat of this Monster is very potent, but like so many of its ilk also very localized. I would strongly recommend that, rather than seeking out this creature, it would be a much wiser course of action merely to shun said beastie.

It would be hugely remiss of me, however, to not suggest some form of defence against it. As a Nation that rules the waves, I would feel terrible to think some sailors had landed in its vicinity and not been educated as to their peril.

Description

The Bandersnatch is primarily a hunting beast. It has no natural predators on its island home, and so has no fear, making it a deadly creature indeed. It is incredibly fleet of foot for such a large animal and on such rocky terrain.

Long powerful bipedal legs allow this creature to literally thunder along, and at rest it stands just over seven feet tall. The legs are located at the rear flanks of the beast, the body is slung almost entirely forward of this position at a slight gradient, only becoming completely horizontal when at a full run. At the rear of the beast is a powerful and articulated tail that it uses for balance during bursts of speed and to entwine and constrict captured prey.

The head of the Bandersnatch is almost the oddest part of all. Its jaws are almost comical in their design and have an array of teeth that criss-cross and overlap to such an alarming degree that its mouth can never fully close. This latter characteristic means that the Bandersnatch constantly has thick, gelatinous saliva strands hanging from its maw and that it makes an alarming whistling noise as it charges down its quarry.

Its eyes are located on either side of its head and are small, red and surrounded by a lumpy callous-like growth. The whole head is lumpen in appearance, being mounted on a neck that the creature can extend, much like a tortoise or terrapin.

The forearms are small and almost useless, and resemble withered featherless wings more than claws or hands. The entire body and head is covered in a thick skin that is deeply and uniformly scored, giving the creature a segmented look, but which in fact allows for more fluid movement.

For a beast with no predators the Bandersnatch is surprisingly violent and seems to delight in carnage and mayhem, practically tearing apart its prey with gay abandon long before it settles down to eat.

If that were not enough, the beast exhales a noxious vapour. Up close this acts as a toxic cloud that paralyses all who breathe it, but the greater risk is the fact that the Bandersnatch tends to live in sheltered caves or hollows, where the toxic fumes build up to a lethal level. The entrance to a lair is more often than not surrounded by the bodies and bones of unfortunate creatures too small to be a meal but who have been overcome by the fumes of what they undoubtedly hoped would be a potential home.

The Bandersnatch are purely carnivorous so will hunt any large creature and will even hunt in rivers and the coastal surf.

Breeding pairs are more numerous than might be thought; this is mainly down to the creature's monogamous nature. Offspring are laid as clutches of eggs; the first hatched devours its rivals – a fine illustration of Mr. Darwin's theory of the survival of the fittest – and the adolescent is then reared by both parents until it is fully grown and moves on to new pastures. Lack of space is the only real limit to their expanding numbers.

Habitat
Rocky island chains with good food supplies.

Bandersnatch

Fig #2

Fig #4

Fig #1

Fig #3

Fig #1 Full body neck retracted
Fig #2 At a run neck extended
Fig #3 Egg with bandage-like shell
Fig #4 Track

Threat

A fearless hunter of all creatures, including Man, it is also crafty, lingering, it seems, at potential port sites around the world. Its veracious appetite and poisonous breath make it a very real threat.

Hunting

The Bandersnatch is a large creature with a violent temper and a thick hide. It should therefore be felled as quickly as possible, for rarely does one get a second shot.

Obviously only a brave or foolhardy huntsman stands before and stares down such a beast, relying on a steady hand and clear killing shot to come out of the encounter alive.

I have turned and run from a charging rhinoceros, only to have a braver companion aim and fire and have the lifeless beast slide to rest at their very feet. Remember, however, that the Bandersnatch is not a charging rhino and has more tricks up its sleeve than an Egyptian theatre conjurer. Even the stoutest of souls must breathe, and just one deep breath of the paralysing vapours can steal the movement from a trigger finger at the crucial moment.

The creature also has an amazing ability to change direction at a second's notice and yet without losing sight of its prey. Unlike other beasts that charge in straight lines, this disorienting, almost bird-like movement is enough to perplex even the most seasoned of gunmen.

Finally, at the end of its charge, it will suddenly turn, propelling itself through 180 degrees and with a whip of its powerful tail. It then either grasps up its prey in that prehensile appendage and runs off with its quarry or smashes them sideways with bone-shattering force.

A sensible man, therefore, will not stand his ground, elephant gun at full cock. A seasoned hunter of the Bandersnatch is a craftier individual by far and will stalk his prey. A beast with no fear is naturally un-skittish in character, so a stalker's approach like that employed by the ghillies of the Scottish estates is particularly effective.

Unfortunately, however honed one's skills as a stalker, it is quite possible that the Bandersnatch may just end up stalking you. Standing so lofty at a height of just over seven feet, it has a good view of the land about and is often scouting for food. A smart hunter, therefore, always knows where his bell is. Curiously, the tone of a common brass bell is enough to startle this creature and force it to retreat far enough away to allow you egress.

In short, a good high-calibre hunting rifle, brass bell, air-filtering mask and ghillie suit are all that is truly needed for hunting the Bandersnatch.

The Achilles' heel, so to speak, of the Bandersnatch is the neck and this is where any gunfire should be aimed. Although it appears to be covered in the same thick hide, the neck skin is closer to the thickness of a pig skin and a few well-placed shots can usually fell the beast with ease. Alternatively, a shot in the neck from behind can enter the skull and fell the beast even faster.

If you are unfortunate enough to be entangled and carried off in the beast's tail, be thankful if you are taken back to the lair (though only if you are wearing an air-filtering mask, of course!). In this instance, the beast intends to consume you later, relying on the vapours within the lair to finish you off. An air-filtering mask will allow you to bide your time and exit when you are free to do so.

Personal Account

It was John Brown who suggested the hunt (I have no understanding of why he was such a favourite of the Queen, as he is an insufferable bore and full of his own self-importance). He had heard of the Bandersnatch and arranged a hunting party made up of himself, a few notable City gentlemen and myself, as an expert in this field.

From the off we were set for disaster, as Brown had mocked my request for air-filtering masks and handbells for all. He had stated that the masks would impair our vision and that one bell was enough, arguing that it could be rung with as much repelling gusto by one, as many could be by a host, and that every ringing bell was one fewer barking gun.

Brown also had a map of our destination that was so devoid of any real useable information it was as good as blank. So we set off past the Scottish islands and out into the chill waters of the North, until eventually we laid anchor at Brown's Island, a place not dissimilar in look to the other craggy carbuncles I had encountered this beast upon. Even from the shore I could see wooded areas,

TIPS

Always hunt in groups — the Bandersnatch
is not a solitary creature and is fast.

Always know where your bell is.

Wear sensible footwear that reaches well
up the calf — the Bandersnatch hunts on
uneven terrain and one wrong step can
twist your ankle and render you unable
to pursue or, more crucially, to escape.

---

gorges and chines that were classic Bandersnatch territory. Around me Brown was readying our hunting party and I could already see a nice array of well-crafted hunting rifles being cleaned and preened.

Our skipper found a nice natural port and we moored and carefully dismounted and huddled together on the beach. I took out my Empire pistol and bell from my travelling case and holstered them both on my belt. Then I slipped my well-worn but comfortable filter mask onto my face. I ignored Brown's derisive guffaw that set chuckles off amongst the party.

Suddenly, beneath the laughter I heard another noise that took a few moments to register as a shrill whistle. Then they were upon us, a whole pack ...

Two were mature beasts, one by its size a bull, and finally a young adolescent. They came at as from around a headland outcrop, their large gait keeping even the younger of the three easily clear of the surf.

I commend the party on how many rifles were brought to bear in such a short time, but the speed of a Bandersnatch is almost impossible to describe and with one pass we had lost three members of our group. A lesser man, in the face of such a crisis, would have given up the hunt forthwith – and that is exactly what Mr. John Brown did.

I, on the other hand, saw that we were now on a rescue mission – three British subjects on foreign soil had been taken and it fell to me to mount a rescue. As was expected, I went without Brown, but I did get to take two braver souls with me, a banker and a member of the clergy, who up to that point had said very little owing to his pronounced stammer.

We set off into the island's interior at a fair pace. The beasts were easy to follow as their whistling seemed to carry on the wind. The moment it stopped so did we. The silence seemed to carry with it a sense of imminent dread.

We soon came upon the lair, which lay low in a craggy gully. The entrance of a dark cave mouth was littered with what appeared to be tiny white sticks, while at the far end the gully itself was sheltered further by a small copse of trees around its upper lip. I motioned to my two companions to remain put amongst the vegetation, and, having checked my face mask, I descended into the cave.

All three of our companions' bodies were laid out on the bone-ridden floor. The fumes were so strong I could smell them through my mask and I could feel my muscles start to cramp. I tried to drag one of the bodies out into the fresh air but my muscles were already overtaken by such a painful torpor that I could barely move my arms. I knew that I would need to abandon the bodies, for dying to save corpses was a pointless action I have only seen American soldiers willing to risk. I was also aware that if the beast's lair was empty, then three very fierce and violent creatures were for some reason waiting nearby.

I exited the cave and crawled back up onto the bank, tearing off my mask, and taking large rasping breaths of fresh air until my limbs stopped burning. I scrambled back up the gorge to the waiting banker and man of the cloth, to whom I related the sorry fate of our fallen comrades. As I spoke, my eyes were constantly drawn to the shoulder of the banker's hunting jacket. I remember asking what it was he had rolled in, and reached forward to wipe away the glistening mess ... It stuck to my fingers and came away in mucus-like strands. My eyes went up to the low tree canopy above us. I spent a while looking at the thick leaves before I saw them standing there ... quietly, chests rising and falling.

I had never been this close to a living Bandersnatch and was suddenly aware how bark-like their skins looked, giving them perfect camouflage amongst the trees. It was here, it seemed, that they slept in the warmish midday sun. I clasped my hand over the banker's mouth, sensing he was about to talk. Unfortunately this meant I wiped mucus across his mouth and he recoiled with a gasp of abject horror.

I saw the bull Bandersnatch's eyes spring open, and in one fluid motion I pulled out my handgun and fired. More by luck I struck him clear in the eye and with a roar he spun and fell crashing down into the gully. The banker disappeared from beside me as the cow's strong tail struck him across the chest and flung him out of my sight. The calf appeared to leap, jaws snapping at the position the banker had flown. The female roared beside me as the clergyman discharged a rifle into its thick chest. I, however, aimed and fired into the neck several times and watched her tumble down onto the floor motionless, eyes wide yet sightless.

Rising to our feet in mere seconds, we heard a rifle discharge and presently came upon the dead body of the calf and the wounded and unconscious body of the banker. His smoking rifle was beside him, its barrel still partially in the beast's mouth. An exit wound gaped at the back of the calf's head. It was three for three.

I can't tell you what happened to those two men after that encounter, but I doubt that they ever trusted that Scotsman, John Brown, again.

Constructs

'And God created man in his image.' ...
Man, on the other hand, just wants to be doing the same trick himself.

Description

In general, Constructs are male and female humans of larger proportions than average, not bulkier as may previously have been thought, just larger. For a Construct actually to function with any clarity, *details* must be present. The more detail, the better a Construct slips into society unnoticed. For this reason, a creator does himself a better service by working to a larger scale.

Constructs can be built from any material; clay or mud was a popular medium for many early creators. Mud, however, dries and breaks, and individual Constructs made from such can often be recognized by the different kinds of mud that have been used to fix them. The mud and clay creations are strong yet slow and ponderous – single-minded beasts that follow simple instructions. Their facial features are so crude as to look more like the suggestion of a face, like something you might see in a rock or cloud formation.

Wooden Constructs seem more popular in North America; they are faster and more cunning but at the same time as simple in form as their mud or clay cousins.

The Construct that offers the most threat, however, is the cadaver. Built from dead flesh and tissue, this Construct combines all the strength of the earthen vessels and all the speed and cunning of the wooden ones, but with the intelligence of Man. Creators also feel they can improve on Nature by adding internal organs or leaving out what they feel is a hindrance. It is far from unusual to find a cadaver with two hearts or greater lungs. Sometimes the pain sensors of the body may be dampened or non-existent, and sometimes even the bone structure will be strengthened.

Whatever the material from which they are built, they are all made animate in the same way – by the introduction of a glowing clear liquid called *shem*. The story is unclear as to its source but legend has it the original shem was formed by the collected tears of the Watchers when they were expelled from Heaven.

Other stories, though, tell of shem being the pure spark of life which brought us all out of the mud. The crucial thing to know, however, is that it can be extracted from the air around us – with the right knowledge and equipment. By an application of electricity in just the right way, one can create and distil shem oneself. Apply it in the right measure to your material and you have life ... of a sort.

Endowed with the right internal organs, a Construct can actually create shem internally. For this to occur, a womblike organ needs to be included within the creature – over the years the body will naturally distil its own life-giving shem.

Habitat

Constructs will generally shun society and so are more likely to be encountered in remote or desolate areas. Obviously they can travel anywhere, so keep your eyes open and your wits about you, Have you *really* looked at that gentleman sitting beside you in the railway carriage?

Threat

Constructs are generally more robust than humans and, since a Construct can (in most cases) be given any instruction, *en masse* they would potentially make an unstoppable army. For this reason alone they are a serious, threat, however benign they may appear.

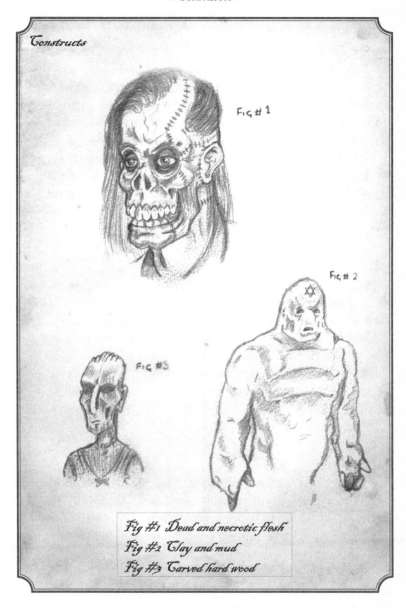

Constructs

Fig # 1

Fig # 2

Fig #3

Fig #1 Dead and necrotic flesh
Fig #2 Clay and mud
Fig #3 Carved hard wood

As we have seen, some Constructs are able to generate more of the life-giving elixir, shem. Because shem can bring life to any inanimate object, Constructs can wield great power.

Hunting

First off, what is the Construct made of? Do not instantly assume that you are faced with flesh and blood. It takes a different mind set to realize that what is actually moving around in front of you is possibly stone, metal or wood. Clay and mud may be common media but they are far from the only ones used. Shem added to a suit of armour has taken a lot of hunters by surprise.

There are two types of weapon I can recommend for hunting the non-flesh Construct. When combatting them at a distance, I can only recommend the solid slug thrower; indeed, any gun that can deliver an *unshaped* round. As long as your munitions do not have a point, you are in luck. You do not need penetration with a Construct; you need something that will *shatter*.

By contrast, if you need to fight a Construct at close hand, I recommend a sharpened sledge hammer, with a good weight and a point. The flesh Construct is like fighting a human being with the addition of a few surprises.

The best way to overcome a Construct is to blind *it*. Once it is unable to see, you can fight on equal terms.

Remember at all times, though, the Construct is an it; they are not men and they are certainly not women. I have seen many a good man go down because they have paused on that trigger come the crucial moment.

Personal Accounts

THE CASE OF AMUN RA

Legends have to come from somewhere, and that is why I was sitting in a café in Egypt with Sir Richard. We had been friends for many years, despite his and my ceaseless travels around the globe. Eventually he had come across a Construct in Egypt and instantly thought of me. The Construct in question – who went under the name of Amun Ra – was especially devious and was hiding behind a group of influential followers.

Posing as a reincarnation of an ancient Egyptian priest, he had promised the people who had discovered him all kinds of impossible futures. These followers had unearthed him in a tomb they

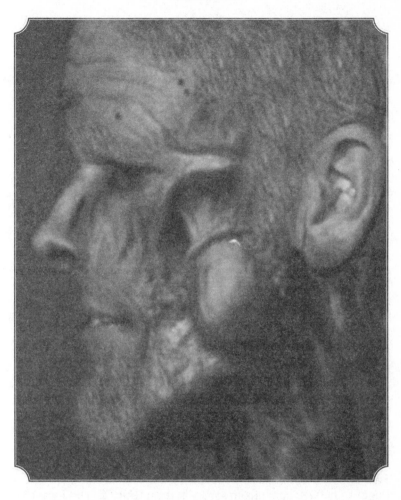

were excavating, completely unaware that he had just been using it as a place to hide from society. Once he had impressed upon them that he could bring them power and riches, they started to bring along other associates. It was at this point that Sir Richard became involved and for some time he managed to keep them believing he had links to the Queen's Secret Service and that he would be able to benefit their leader in some way.

In the café he described the Construct to me. He sounded an ugly brute – he was six foot tall and with yellowed cracked skin through which you could see the veins and the muscles working beneath. At that moment two men approached our table and sat down. Neither was much over five and a half foot so I knew that neither of them was the Construct. From their appearance they looked Egyptian but they remained silent. Richard drank his thick coffee and looked at them for a while, also not talking, until finally a third person sat down.

He was wearing traditional gear that concealed most of his appearance from prying eyes. I smiled for the outlandish garb actually made him stand out more, especially as Sir Richard and I were dressed in very British linen suits, and so were not the natural drinking partners of such a man. As he sat down, the two other men got up and walked away, to skulk once more in the street outside I imagined.

Amun Ra spoke very well, with an accent that I couldn't quite place, and proceeded to vaunt, in a style almost akin to a salesman's patter, the wonders he could promise the Empress of India if I could furnish him with an introduction. I listened carefully to his words, occasionally having to turn to Richard for translations of certain Egyptian phrases. When he had finished, we all sat quietly for some moments.

I then explained to him, in fairly hushed tones, my country's knowledge of what he was. I gave him a stark choice: he would either have to leave with us now and return to England where we would look after him; or we would end his life right there and then, even in front of all those people smoking and drinking coffee in the café. He was a sensible creature and decided on the first option and recommended we leave through the back of the café so as to shake off his Egyptian bodyguards. Amun Ra, Sir Richard and I went into the back alley where we took a few turns to get away from the general hubbub.

I think Amun Ra was surprised when the first blade severed his spine. We managed to dispose of the body quite cleanly. I had known from the moment that the two bodyguards had sat at our table that we couldn't dispatch him in the café as we had intended. It was easy to use the Construct's natural paranoia and arrogance against him and get him to lead us somewhere quiet. As I have said, shem is a potent threat to the Empire and the vessels in which it is created are Monsters pure and simple. Sometimes I do not like my job but it is still a job that needs doing.

THE CASE OF 'THE RIPPER'

London 1888. You all know the date; you all know the crime, at least as it was reported in the broadsheets. However, the fact is stranger than the fiction.

I am sorry to dispel the myth but there was no single ripper. I enjoyed writing the 'Dear Boss' letter and that postcard; however, they had a serious purpose – to throw the newspapermen and the police off the scent of the real crimes being committed in Whitechapel.

A gang had been working the Whitechapel's prostitutes for almost a year, using their murdered bodies to harvest organs. I had heard initially about the affair through my mother's contacts and had taken the time to get together a team of Dragons to find out more. [The Royal Order of Dragons existed primarily on British soil, righting society's wrongs and, much like most societies of the time, preferred secrecy. I could happily count myself a member.]

We had tracked the gang down to an area just outside of Greenwich, south of the river, and found they were in the employ of a Dr. Lucas Bargeman. A former Dragon himself, he had discovered the properties of shem during a case but had kept it to himself. Because he thought prostitutes the lowest of the low, and had no compassion for their sufferings, he saw them as a cheap source of body parts and organs. Bargeman had been a slave-runner from Dahomey to New Orleans and on one trip had managed to acquire four of King Ghezo's Mino – an expert group of muscular, highly trained and disciplined female warriors of huge stature as part of a deal. Unable to sell them in the Americas, he brought them back to England where he promptly killed them with poison and used their preserved cadavers in his medical experiments. Later on, after the discovery of shem, he started to rebuild the women. By this point, some body parts were missing and that's where the London gang came in.

TIPS

Work out the Constructs material then
play to its weaknesses — for instance, wood
burns, stone shatters and flesh bleeds.

Flesh Constructs get sentimental — work
with this. Treachery is only treacher-
ous when done to your own species.

No Construct can drown, so do not try this.

Always try to lure your Construct to
areas of extreme cold; this will not kill
them but because they do not have any
body heat it slows them down.

Never feel tempted to use the shem on yourself
— the risks are too great.

I include this story because I need the reader to be aware that Constructs are a threat but we need to be just as wary of the creators also.

We descended on force into Bargeman's laboratories and were met with a charnel house of gruesome body parts. As the building was guarded by Bargeman's gang and three resurrected Mino, we had our work cut out for us.

The gang was made up of dockworkers and they had a mean streak but no real flare for tactics. I saw at least two go down when they burst from cover in an attempt to charge professionally armed men. The Mino, however, were trained warriors and Bargeman had made sure he had enhanced his works of art to the maximum. I saw an old friend die when one of the Constructs flew at least ten foot into the air from a standing jump and landed on him with an iklwa — a short Zulu spear — which pierced straight into his heart.

We managed to kill only one of the Constructs; the other two escaped into the night and I have never found them, though I have heard tales of statuesque ebony warrior women from around the world ever since.

Bargeman, on the other hand, was caught, lobotomized and left in the Bedlam.

I chuckle to myself every time I read a new, far-fetched theory about The Ripper. Oh if only they knew how far-fetched the truth was!

Ghoti

I would love to take credit for naming this beast, but unfortunately that honour must go to our riverboat captain – a former Oxford scholar who lived his retirement years running the mighty Amazon in his steam-powered sloop *The Empire Ghost*. He had come to South America in order to continue his ichthyologic studies, for the Amazon had unlimited undiscovered fish for him to catalogue. As he rightly said of the monster he named: 'This is a fish all right but you wouldn't know for looking at it.' For non Oxford scholars I recommend researching the name Ghoti to understand the joke.

Description

The Ghoti measures between five and six foot, although it must be noted that, when out of water, they often become stooped under their own weight so may appear deceptively shorter.

Coloration seems to match that of the fish life in the area, so generally brown, greens and mottled greys predominate. However, more vibrant colours have been reported as well as interesting chameleon effects, as seen in some flatfish and octopi.

The head is slightly larger than a human skull, flanked either side by large gill flaps and powerful neck muscles. The mouth is wide, lipless and full of a replenishing array of hooked needle-like teeth.

The eyes appear lifeless at all times and, containing just a pupil, are more fluid than the human eye. The forehead is surmounted with a raised bump that is used in sonar location underwater.

Feet and hands both display signs of lengthened digits that are heavily webbed to allow speedy propulsion through the water and to some extent on soft or boggy terrain, acting somewhat like a snowshoe. They are also not averse to travelling on four limbs, much like a toad, and can leap along at a speed equivalent to a fast walk.

The body of the Ghoti is solidly built, although lithe. I would be more than happy to compare it to my old friend Captain Webb who took it upon himself to swim the Channel. However, Old Webby was not covered in rough scales and odd flukes like the Ghoti.

Ghoti show many signs of intelligence and, although they appear like simple creatures, they have been observed in social interaction, using basic tools and in some cases, adornment. It must be said that individuals who have been infected may be responsible for some of these reports as they go through the process of changing into full Ghoti.

Ghoti tend to make nests close to the shore of their haunts. These are recognizable as shallow indents worn into rocks or pushed into the mud. The nest will be strewn with the detritus of the Ghoti's aquatic diet and may consist of shells, water weeds, fish and aquatic mammal bones.

Ghoti tend to hunt alone but not exclusively so – they can often be part of a large offshore pod that may be as much as twenty to thirty strong. However, a rich food source would have to be available to support such large numbers.

Habitat

Ghoti range across the globe and breeds have been sighted, swimming and hunting, in many different inland waterways and coastal areas, Scotland, Ireland, Cornwall and Devon seem to have the most sightings here at home, often giving rise to myths of selkies, mermaids, kelpies and formori.

Elsewhere in the world, they may be seen in many remote island chains, the hidden lagoons of the Amazon, the seas of Japan

Ghoti

Fig # 1

Fig # 2

Fig # 3

Fig # 4

Fig #1 On land
Fig #2 Detail of head
Fig #3 Track
Fig #4 Skull with forehead holes for sonar

(although generally of a larger scale there) and, for some reason, in the isolated inlets of the American west coast.

Threat

You may well wonder why I consider this creature a Monster. Well, the answer is simple yet scary. It would appear that, although Ghoti breed naturally, they also have another way of increasing their numbers.

The world of science has suggested that several breeds of fish and amphibian can change sex in times of need to increase the species. Ghoti, on the other hand, have an enzyme they excrete which, if it gets into the human blood stream, actually starts to change the human into one of them. Some cultures actually imbibe Ghoti blood ritually in order to change themselves into the creatures they admire and worship. Another worrying fact is that the enzyme can lay dormant in a female host but become active in any offspring she may have. This makes these creatures a threat to all human life, and therefore, by definition, Monsters.

Hunting

The Ghoti are obviously both land-dwelling and aquatic creatures, so therefore pose a series of hunting challenges. Unfortunately, owing to the Ghoti's dexterous digits (understandably not seen in most aquatic denizens), fishing equipment is not as effective as might be hoped, so you might as well leave the poles and home-tied flies at home in the hunting lodge.

However, fishing spears or tridents are good simple weapons if hunting whilst submerged. But, best of all, a good stock of dynamite will help bring most lagoon-dwelling Ghoti to the surface and therefore within the sights of a good hunting rifle.

When employing a rifle, be aware that hard, scale-like plates makes up the mass of the Ghoti's hide. The weak points are the softer lower abdomen from the bottom of the sternum to the groin (often helpfully lighter in colour), the gills, the underarm joint, the backs of the knees, the mouth and eyes. If engaged in direct contact with a blade or handgun, try to strike upwards, as this blow is more likely to penetrate beneath the overlapping plates.

If you find yourself in the water, take a deep breath and swim to the bottom and then drag yourself to the shore. Underwater,

Ghoti rely primarily on a form of sonar to locate their prey. If you are on the bottom, you will be harder to find and the debris you throw up into the water as you crawl will also add to your cover. If you are in a close-contact tussle with a Ghoti, then it is worth knowing that the sonar is located in the bump-like protrusion on the forehead – a swift blow to this protrusion and your Ghoti is incapacitated for several seconds.

Personal Accounts
THE HUNT OF THE AMAZONIAN LAGOON MONSTER

I had not hunted the Ghoti before my trip up the Amazon on *The Empire Ghost* but here I was, about one mile away from our camp, crouched at the side of a deep, evil-smelling lagoon.

It wasn't the hottest of nights I had spent in the jungle but it was definitely getting close. Sitting back from the edge of the lagoon, I watched the swarms of mosquitoes skimming across the surface highlighted by the cool bluish light of the moon. I closed my mouth tight every time the buzzing got closer to my position, so as not to attract them over with the odour of my own hot breath.

Tonic water may well give one a certain immunity to infection but its flavour seems to attract the insects like honey attracts bees and, although I was glad to fend off the sleeping sickness, I sometimes wondered if that wouldn't be preferable to being awake nights on end cursed with that insistent itching.

The only thing that made the situation of crouching in the undergrowth bearable was watching as the pale-skinned hunter, who had journeyed out with me to the lagoon side, swatted and swished at the clouds of bugs that had set up permanent residence around him. Although the waving arms may have been alerting our prey to his presence, I was more than happy to see the bugs were over there with him and not over with me.

The water's surface broke beneath a large cloud of bugs and an audible smack filled the still air as a lipless mouth slammed shut, then the fish was gone leaving a huge circle of ripples expanding across the water's surface. I took aim at the next big cloud of insects, the previous having been dispersed or eaten. Glancing round, I saw my hunting colleague pointing at the same cloud and that quick lapse of concentration was enough.

For a moment the flash of my companion's elephant gun stole my night vision and the weapon's retort echoed around the glade, filling it with reverberating noise and the cacophony of jungle sounds, as the trees came alive with the chatter of monkeys and the screech of a myriad of birds.

The water sprayed up in front of me and I was knocked over from my crouched position as a beast erupted from the fetid water and barrelled into the enveloping undergrowth. It was my first sight of a Ghoti, but, still blinking away the lights before my eyes, I could only recall its solid mass and a pungent smell. I rolled over onto my belly and let off a volley of shots into the surrounding jungle, in the vain hope that the beast would be struck by chance.

Then I was on my feet and running, aware that the creature could be enraged and that it was travelling in the direction of the camp and the young ladies. These girls had been a welcome distraction during the initial part of our journey but had become somewhat of an encumbrance since the jungle had thickened and the temperature had risen to dizzying heights during the day.

I was surprised to hear the undergrowth at my left-hand side splintering, and again I was barrelled to the ground and rolled end over end several times before coming to a stop against a stump. I still held on to my Empire gun but was painfully aware that it had only two shots left in the barrel — another unguided volley would leave me virtually unarmed to any sensible degree.

The beast was standing not far away, its shoulders heaving as it seemed to drag in great rasping gulps of air. Its head was held low, making it seem headless, its form still only an outline from my recumbent position. Slowly I started to stand, bringing my pistol level and bracing my arms against the kick. Suddenly the undergrowth erupted behind me and my elephant-gun-wielding partner shot off past me at a tangent, too excited by the unseen chase to realize it had, in fact, already come to a standstill.

The outburst, however, prompted the Ghoti to charge. My gun recoiled with the first shot and, as training had always dictated, another bullet quickly followed the first home. The beast spun round, as the only shot to hit home whirled it on its axis. Ichor decorated the branches and broad leaves directly behind the beast as it sank down to the jungle floor. It was like watching a balloon deflate after a naughty child has let all the air out.

The creature itself had two large-calibre holes in its chest and both were exuding a foul-smelling substance. My hunting companion returned and we slung our quarry between us and returned to camp, where our Oxford-trained riverboat Captain examined the brute and was pleased to tell us that we had brought down a female that was rich with eggs.

Buoyed by this happy event, we stayed several more weeks in the area looking for a male but unfortunately did not find one. One day, I imagine, another expedition will come out to this dark lagoon but without the presence of a breeding pair their chances of getting a decent hunt of their own will be slim.

TIPS

Remember to wear lightweight clothing, as you
may at some stage end up in the water. Clothing
will weigh you down and make you an easier
target for creatures used to hunting in water.

Never hunt alone — Ghoti are not exclusively
solitary creatures and therefore could take a
lone hunter by surprise with ease.

Keep your eyes open at all times as Ghoti have
natural camouflage and are good stalkers.

Take a local guide with you who knows
the land well as watery areas often have
many hidden natural hazards.

THE HUNT OF THE SCOTTISH ISLAND MONSTERS

I include this account as a contrast to the account of hunting
Ghoti in inland waterways just related. As I have already stated,
Ghoti also dwell in coastal regions and by this point I had hunted
several of both types. However, I feel this particular expedition
was interesting for several reasons.

I was instructed to journey to the Outer Hebrides to the
Flannan Isles, known locally as the 'Seven Hunters'. It is an old
pilgrimage site to the chapel of St. Flannan, who, as I recall, was an
Irish bishop. The islands had been pretty much empty of human
occupation for many years and it was only the possible use of the
islands as a site for a new lighthouse that had aroused any curiosity.

I travelled out with my batman Kent and two local fishermen, as
guides to the islands. We took ten whaling harpoons (trust me, I had
my reasons after a Japanese trip), four barbed tridents, two elephant

guns and a box of dynamite, as well as enough camping equipment to keep the four of us comfortable on the islands for two months.

The islands are very rough and ready. Locals bring sheep over to graze and grow fat, with no fear of predators. Kent got quite partial to puffin meat as we spent our days scouting out the island chain and I often found myself distracted by the dolphins that frolicked offshore.

The reason for our trip was a local story told by the shepherds and fishermen. Rumours had it that men had been going missing from the islands for many years, taken by creatures of the sea that came up onto the land. The disappearance of a surveyor from the Northern Lighthouse Board was where we came in. After six weeks of searching we were convinced all disappearances were due to the sudden and rough seas. All four of us had watched several sheep suddenly washed out to sea and drowned on what had hitherto appeared to be a calm day; we had even had several near misses of our own.

So by this stage we had turned the whole trip into more of a jolly than a serious hunt. I was out net-fishing with William, the eldest of our local companions, when I thought I saw some strange movement in a cave. William tried to get us closer but the tides would not allow it without some danger, so, remembering our dynamite, we decided to flush anything out of the cave with a blast.

I steadied the boat whilst he lit the dynamite stick and got ready to pitch the explosive into the cave. Before he could do so, our boat met with a violent jerk from beneath and the dynamite ended up in our keel. I took my cue and dived from the boat into the surf, expecting William to follow suit. I can only believe he tried to recover the explosive stick from the boat but in vain, for the blast that sank our craft was a macabre mix of wood and William.

I immediately knew what our foe was, for I had met such tactics before. The water was cold and dark but the Ghoti that now appeared beside me seemed oblivious, consumed as it was by a desire to kill. Its mouth was open so wide that my hand could have disappeared inside without touching the sides.

As I struggled in the water, my fingers brushed against the

fishing net that we had previously cast into the water. I snatched it up and swung it in front of me, surprised to catch not one but two attacking Ghoti in its weave. Their natural camouflage had made them almost invisible in the murk. However, I quickly realized that I was entangled in the net and that all three of us were being pushed towards the rocks, a mass of writhing, snapping fury that I knew would smash my body to smithereens. The prospect scared me into brutal action.

I snatched at some broken debris from the explosion and stabbed repeatedly at anything that flashed within the net ... eyes, gills, anything that moved. After what seemed an eternity of stolen breaths, frantic stabbing and foul-tasting water I managed to free myself and clambered onto a craggy outcrop, dragging the net with its now-lifeless catch up behind me.

I waited for some time before Kent and Samuel found me, attracted to my location by the explosion. We had to leave the net behind, as we could not manoeuvre it into the boat, and as we sailed away again we watched the gulls as they picked at the carcasses within.

We returned later that day to say words for William and then seal the cave entrance with better-placed dynamite; we spent the rest of our time on the island more alert but saw no further sign of the Ghoti. To my knowledge, no one else has since gone missing from the islands.

Jabberwock

I must admit, ever since I have been hunting Monsters for the Crown and for the protection of the Empire, I have always wanted to be given the mission of hunting down a Dragon. I have never met one yet, but feel there must be such creatures out there. I cannot believe, given the variety of beasts I have encountered, that the numerous tales of this winged, fire-breathing beast are mere legend.

It is therefore with great relish that I can tell you about the Jabberwock — for a would-be Dragon-slayer like myself, nothing could come closer.

Description
This is a monstrous beast, fearsome, full of spite and rage in the heat of battle, but also one of our most solitary foes, keeping itself aloof from any other form of life. Like the crocodile, it seems to need to feed rarely as its digestion is slow and sluggish, and it has very little need to use much energy.

The creature itself at full height must be close on fifteen foot tall. It has a long articulated neck and likewise a long articulated tail. At full stretch, you are looking at a beast that nears twenty foot in length with ease — if you include the tail.

The main body is pear-like in shape, giving the impression of a bloated belly that tapers towards the shoulders. It stands on powerful hind legs which have the largest claws I have ever seen on a beast; they are easily a foot in length. The shoulders sprout human-like arms, muscular and sinewy, and ending in four feather-covered claws that look almost like a cluster of slender Turkish daggers.

The back has two sets of bat-like wings; they are too small for flight or hovering but seem to be used as a cooling aid much like an elephant will flap its ears. The wings are very often torn and ragged, suggesting little in the way of nerve endings, but heavy veins can be seen pulsing in them when the Jabberwock is excited or exerting itself.

The head of the Jabberwock is astonishing and I confess to know only three men who have trophy Jabberwock heads in their very private collections. The head is about the size of a human torso and is somewhat elongated, rather like the head of a horse. Its mouth is fronted by what can only be described as an enormous rodent-like overbite.

In fact, the Jabberwock has only four rectangular teeth in total – two in the upper jaw and a slightly smaller pair in the lower. Towards the very back of the mouth it has four large grinding slabs, two top and two bottom, spread either side. These slabs are not teeth but merely ridged bone.

The Jabberwock's eyes are huge and take up a large proportion of the head. The pupils are tiny, and surrounded by a sun-like iris of the brightest bloody red. The main expanse of the eye is a swirling creamy liquid that is most nauseating to look at. The eyes themselves are protruding and bulging, and if Mr. Darwin's theories are to be believed, this must be accounted a horrible design flaw to have lingered for so many generations.

The jowls of the face sprout many feelers, starting with two rather prominent ones, like those found on a catfish, leading into a series of more whisker-like ones. The top of the head is surmounted by two long thin twisting horns.

The Jabberwock skin is dark brown in colour and made up of large overlapping scaly plates.

The beast itself makes a burbling sound as if it is blowing bubbles in the back of its throat; this cry changes to a higher

Jabberwock

Fig # 1

2½ FT

Fig # 3

Fig #2

Fig #1 The Jabberwock at full height, wings unfurled
Fig #2 Detail of head
Fig #3 Tracks

resonance just before it attacks. The sound is constant and stops only upon death, a good indicator of a kill.

Habitat

The Jabberwock lives in heavily wooded areas and relies a lot on subterranean cavern systems for shelter and secrecy. This means that countries offering the right kind of terrain and habitat are few and far between. The solitary nature of the Jabberwock also limits its habitat.

Jabberwocks have also been sighted on many uninhabited islands, mainly in temperate regions.

Threat

The threat to the Empire does not come from the beast itself; it is merely a predator. The true threat comes from another matter altogether. The Jabberwock has a gland inside its head that when consumed in its entirety gives the gourmet a non-degenerative cellular system, in short, halting the ageing process. This in the hands of the wrong individual could be disastrous for the Empire. On the other hand, it could also be hugely advantageous to the Empire if we get there first. It would be remiss of me to reveal who has already eaten of the 'Jabberwock fruit'.

Hunting

It is a strange world indeed where it is easier to be hunted and defend yourself until victorious, than it is to actually go on a hunt.

To hunt a Jabberwock in its subterranean lair is possibly the last mistake you will ever make. Being a large creature, the Jabberwock, when in tunnels, lies flat on its belly and crawls. It backs itself into the tunnels and therefore any hunter going into their lair will be faced only by biting jaws and claws designed to catch and hold prey, not to mention those huge eyes used to seeing in the gloom. With this in mind, your best course of action is to wait for the creature to emerge above ground.

Such a rare occurrence is the Jabberwock hunt, however, that it is an unfortunate fact that you must wait until a Jabberwock attack is reported and then get to the location as fast as you can to play the hopeful next victim.

Once in the area of a reported attack, you just need make

TIPS

Hold your blade as if on ceremonial parade — this
will inspire you to strike up and under the scales.

The wings and eyes are the only unprotected
area and should be attacked whenever possible to cause blood loss and pain.

Always remain armoured, however
uncomfortable you may become.

The horns are purely for show and therefore
need not be feared or protected against. They
are brittle and constantly grow and break.

Hunt alone — faced with such rewards you want
to be wrestling only with your own morals.

---

yourself available. The Jabberwock is indiscriminate in its choice
of prey and will hunt for around five days before disappearing
once again. Hunts happen at around six-month periods, but do not
fall into the trap of thinking that if you miss a hunt it is merely a
question of waiting in the same place until six months have passed.
These beasts have multiple hunting grounds, meaning it could be
many years before they return to a region.

Now you are ready for an attack, you merely need to travel the
area looking for the distinctive gouge marks and tracks left by the
large hind claws. Keep your ears keen for the distinctive bubbling
noise and general sounds of crashing through foliage.

You should be equipped as close to the apparel and weaponry
of a knight as your conscience will allow. The overlapping scales
seem to deflect most bullets and the teeth are so large as to block

a clear shot into an open mouth. The eyes are admittedly a very tempting target, but a shot to the head in this manner will destroy the brain and the precious gland, so is a last form of attack only.

A sword is the best weapon to use here and preferably one with a long, thin blade that can penetrate deep beneath the scales if used in upward thrusts. Since the Jabberwock uses slashing and biting moves, a form of hard-wearing clothing or, better still, an armoured vest of some kind will protect the vital organs of your torso, while a simple pith helmet will deflect most blows to the head.

The Jabberwock will generally favour two forms of attack. The first is a kind of 'leap and devour' manoeuvre. The beast will jump up into the air using its degenerative wings to give it extra lift, before extending its neck fully and leading with its devastating bite, targeting vulnerable areas such as the head or limbs. A single bite this way can remove a limb in its entirety and the resulting shock and blood loss will usually kill a victim with a fair amount of speed.

This move is easy to anticipate to the trained hunter. The moment the Jabberwock is airborne, run towards it and dive forward. Since the beast calculates its leap so that it will land exactly at the feet of its prey, or slightly beyond, and once launched it cannot shorten this attack. Your run and dive will take you beneath the Jabberwock and a roll back to your feet will allow you to attack a fairly unguarded back. With a few well-aimed swipes with a blade, you can remove the wings and start blood loss, rendering the creature incapable of another leap attack.

The second form of attack is the catch and bite. The Jabberwock swings its strong forearms in a scissor movement and ensnares its prey in long fingers tipped with its razor-sharp hooked claws. If caught in this way, the body is usually transfixed and the victim incapable of escape without further damage.

The reaction to this pinning movement is more often than not the natural one of jumping back, but this only helps to impale the prey further. Knowing this, you have to override your impulse and leap forward into the creature's belly, preferably with an un-sportsman-like raised knee. The impact will open the creature's arms.

Use your close approximation to strike upwards with your sword, allowing it to penetrate beneath the scales and upward into the internal organs of the Jabberwock's chest cavity. Three blows should be enough to cause a significant bleed and damage. When time allows, the Jabberwock should be rendered blind with two very easy sword swipes to the eyes. Then it is purely a case of avoiding the creature as it dies, aiming any free blows at the neck. Caution, though. Never get too close – the eyes are blind but the creature still has the feelers that sprout from its lower jaw, and the moment they brush anything warm it will strike out in that direction.

The moment the beast has died, remove the head. The fruit is inside but should remain there until it has reached the intended consumer.

Personal Account

There was only one feeling I had as I entered the region. Excitement. I was dressed in fairly warm clothes, as frost was still heavy on the ground, even though the sun was high in the sky. The heat the pale sun emanated only seemed to produce a clinging cold mist from the frozen soil. I pulled my Cossack-style coat closer around me and cursed my metal cuirass that was taking on the cold even through the thick fur.

On my head I wore my trusty pith; it had kept me cool in hotter climes but now I needed it for warmth, so I had dipped it in a stream and let the moisture freeze on the outside, giving me a nice all-over coating that was helping to keep the warmth of my head trapped in its dome. On my eyes I wore hooded goggles to keep the frost's glare to a minimum and I had a Bedouin scarf around my lower face. I was aware that my whole body – and particularly my pith-covered head –was steaming as I walked,

It is sometimes difficult, when the blood is rising and the senses are heightened, not to succumb to the beauty all around you. The trees were devoid of leaves and sparkled in the noonday sun and frost. As I watched the curving flight of a bird of prey I did not recognize, I heard the oncoming sound of my stalker, for, remember, here I was the prey. I drew my sword and because I am a cautious man I also pulled my main-gauche, which is primarily a parrying weapon but with enough of a blade to wound, if not to kill.

I stayed as still as my excitement would allow, uncovering my ears to the chill air, pinpointing the direction of the sound by slowly turning my head back and forth. Then I turned and braced myself.

I could see its approach for a while, although I did not make out its true appearance until it entered the clearing fully. For all my research into this creature, I was not truly ready for it in the flesh. My blood ran cold. Milky-white eyes focused on you, moving as if full of liquid, bring a nausea to your throat. The rodent teeth, when scaled up to monster size, rotten and broken, fill you with a primeval dread that knots your bowels. 'Burbling' sounds comical on paper but in reality it is the sound that a dying man makes when his throat is rent.

I waited in stillness too long and it lunged for me, its arms shooting past me making the prey in me fly, my instinct drawing me backwards at speed. Its claws tore into my clothes and held me tightly; I felt the pressure on the cuirass beneath and suddenly praised God for the uncomfortable garment.

The head shot forward and I brought my main-gauche up into a milky-white eye, showering myself with goo. The Jabberwock threw its head back, letting out a bellow that words alone cannot describe and I took the chance to slip out from my coat, leaving the thick fur tangled in the creature's sharp claws.

It turned its good eye on me and I threw my main-gauche with an accuracy I would have been proud of had it not turned at the last moment, so that the blade clattered off its teeth, cracking one alarmingly.

Its hands became ever more tightly entangled in the shreds of the fur coat. It bit into the tattered fur and the garment finally fell away. The creature yelped as the cracked tooth finally shattered, leaving a jagged stump. What had once been a terrible visage suddenly became a horrific nightmare. Ichor dripped down its ruined face and its mouth was a jagged mess. Its claws, covered in the tatters of fur, now looked like paws and its terrifying burble changed in pitch to almost a scream. It made its final launch.

Despite every instinctive thought in my head telling me to flee, I ran directly at the Jabberwock, diving low and jabbing up with my blade as its vast weight flew overhead. To my horror, however, the blade snagged and was pulled from my grip. I rolled and came to my feet, now weapon-less but for the first time with the tactical advantage. I leapt over the snaking tail and landed amongst the leathery wings, gaining purchase easily.

The creature once again let out the bone-chilling noise, tossing its head backwards. I grabbed one of the twisted horns and wrenched. I was surprised at how difficult it seemed to break, but at last it came free and I span it in my hand and plunged its sharpened point again and again into the soft neck. The Jabberwock's body buckled and I was thrown to the floor, the force of the fall dislodging both my pith and goggles.

I got unsteadily to my feet and took a step forward towards the creature to deliver the *coup de grace*. It turned its eye upon me and for a moment I saw something there that seemed like intelligence, the kind you see in the face of an old man close to death. I pulled forth my sword, which was still embedded in its chest, but the creature did not react. It just continued to burble quietly, seeming to become heavier and heavier before my eyes.

I pushed the blade up and that light in its eye went out. The body fell like a rotten tree, tipping away from me, my blade sliding free. I cannot tell you who I took that head to for in all honesty I do not know; I merely did my job. If I had had any desire to eat that fruit myself, they all faded when I saw that sad ancient light in the Jabberwock's eye.

Jub Jubs

Religion will frequently take us to the Empire's outer most points. Upon reflection, I realise that at these places, having turned my eyes to the heavens, I have more often found the need to suddenly duck rather than offer up praise. So, for everyone who says religious ceremonies should be carried out in God's majesty, under open skies, I can only say 'Try that in Jub Jub country'.

Description

The Jub Jub is a giant predatory bird standing close on eighteen foot tall. The legs are tall, bare and scaled like that of a chicken, ending in elongated, splayed talons that provide great stability and enable large prey to be grasped and carried away. The plumage around the top of the creature's legs is thick, giving the bird the characteristics of wearing lace-bottomed bloomers: as are sometimes seen at the beach huts along Margate seafront.

The bird's body is slight with a muscular chest and heavy weave of feathers. From the body sprout two monumental wings and a swooping neck like that of the common heron. The neck is topped by a crested head with a thick powerful beak. The beak is dark in colour and decorated with bright eye-like markings about halfway along its length. During territorial fights the birds mistakenly peck at these markings, and thus their less obvious dark eyes set high back in the relatively small head are protected.

Plumage varies with location but along its back it will more likely tend towards a broken mottled effect, making them difficult to spot against a leafy canopy from the air. The belly is a lighter version of the back and less mottled. During certain times of the year the male birds sprout a ruff or mane of colourful feathers that I have been assured look elegant in a lady's Sunday hat.

Jub Jubs have an exceptionally long breeding period so there are often nests with eggs and all the problems this implies – protective parents, predatory reptiles and a continued spread of numbers leading to more extensive feeding areas. On the upside Jub Jub eggs make splendidly rich and filling omelettes.

The call of the Jub Jub carries over vast distances and there are two very different sounds: first, the deep, booming 'whupp-whupp' produced by the males and, second, the bone-chilling, fox-like scream used when hunting.

Jub Jubs will take any large prey but prefer long pigs, apes and monkeys. They employ a standard form of snatch-and-drop hunting, allowing them to weaken their prey and also tenderize the upcoming meal. The beaks, although deadly and sharp, seem to be more used for cutting through dead meat and for the afore-mentioned territorial battles.

Habitat

The Jub Jub prefers the thick canopy roofs of jungles and rain forests. Large old trees provide superb, stable nesting grounds for these gigantic creatures, predominantly in the southern hemisphere, but also stretching high up along the African west coast.

Threat

As we take our God to ... I refuse to say godless savages since in most cases they have more gods than I have great-aunts, so instead I will say 'peoples with religions in need of simplification', we, more often than not, have had to send our brave missionaries to remote jungles around the globe. It would be terribly remiss to spend so much time on theological 'simplification', merely to have the entire congregation appear as Jub Jub pellets scattered across the forest floor.

Jub jub

FAKE
EYES ON
BEAK

FIG #2

FIG #1

FIG #4

ESS LOOKS
LIKE POCKMARKED
BURNT CERAMIC

FIG #3

Fig#1 Detail of head
Fig#2 In Flight
Fig #3 Height against average
human
Fig#3 Egg
(like pockmarked burnt ceramic)

Hunting

So where to hunt? Well, the obvious answer is in a jungle area with lots of indigenous people and wildlife. The noisier the place gets at night, the more likely you have got a good hunting ground.

Ask the locals, although this can inspire mistrust, as in some areas the birds have been mixed in with an already full melting pot of tree gods, earth spirits and wind deities and are both feared and worshipped.

Offering trade to most villages will not only provide you with reliable guides but a good team to carry gear and provisions. (By the by I have often found that the local women of Mexico make a very tasty cocoa nut drink that can be livened up with a drop of rum.) If you are not lucky enough to be led straight to a nesting site, then you are going to focus your search down to certain areas. Narrow, dark valleys often make for the strongest, tallest trees and therefore good nesting sites. Subsequently, you could try emulating the territorial booming of the male through a conical horn or ear trumpet and listen for replies. Moreover, when close to a site, you will find broken branches littering the floor from high in the canopy and may find remnants of meals hung from branches, although this is unlikely as the jungle has a host of creatures ready to clear up after a tasty kill.

Once you have discovered your nest area, you should begin to see the large birds in the canopy. This is a time when caution should be at the upmost, for, although big birds, they are amazingly adept at sweeping through the tight trunks and heavy vegetation almost silently, up till the last moment when they will let out that scream that makes every part of you wish to bolt for cover.

Good hunting parties are a must, as the birds do not hunt alone but pass through in small formations. Large-bore rifles are the best weapon, and shots should be aimed at the head, neck and wings, as the body is too heavily feathered and muscled from the front and underside. Shots from behind have more chance of penetrating the overlapping feathers. After a pass, spin around for a final parting shot.

If you happen to be snatched up in a pass, hang on as tight as you can and if possible try to lash yourself to the leg. Although strong, most Jub Jubs cannot carry a full-sized man for very long and will need to land, saving you the embarrassment and pain of a fall.

Once the bird has been grounded, a heavy blow to the underside

of the beak with the butt of a rifle will force the head back, thereby breaking the neck.

Personal Account

I remember being excited when I was asked to go on a Jub Jub hunt near a South American settlement that had been praising the Christian God for almost ten years.

I was excited, not on account of the beautiful jungles of the Amazon basin, not even for the chance to speak to the Indians of the area and to ask about their monster legends. I was actually excited to be going with two legendary learned gentlemen: Charles Kingsley, an author and clergyman I had practically grown up with, but never met, and Alfred Newton, a zoologist who had actually written letters to the Queen condoning my actions.

My brief was to take the gentlemen to the nesting ground and conduct a cull, but in a way that allowed both men to study the animals in relative safety.

The problems started with Newton not taking to me at all and showing an even greater distain for my batman, Kent. I was concerned about Newton's lame leg on the uneven terrain and told him this in no uncertain terms. Then, when we arrived at the

TIPS

Jub Jubs are not easily distracted from
their quarry so do not waste time trying to lure them in your direction.

Jub Jubs are prepared to take desperate risks
in a pursuit, so you can often ground them
by leading into a heavily wooded area.

You will spend a lot of time gazing upwards
on a Jub Jub hunt, but never forget there are
always other dangers at ground level too — from
a branch in the face to a jaguar at the jugular.

Burning Jub Jub feathers will actually deter
their attack — a handful of feathers beside your
campfire will allow you some rest from a hunt.

Always take a machete into the
jungle to clear a path.

---

village in which stood the British mission and in which we were
to make our base camp, Newton retired immediately to his room,
not wishing to mix with the Indians. The proud folk of the village (who now, rather mistakenly, saw themselves as British) took
this slight badly and we ended up with inexperienced guides and
young village hunters who were still looking to make their mark.

Kingsley, however, had been a dream the entire voyage and the
moment we reached the village he was happily giving sermons and
learning about the nature of the jungle around us. Once again,
however, I was concerned about my companion's mobility in the
terrain, as his declining years were starting to show.

We left early one morning. Kent and I took an advanced lead, mainly so as to seek out an easier route and to clear a path. It was an arduous task, and by day fifteen even my patient batman was starting to show signs of strain, and talk around the campfire would often sound as if we were planning on touring the whole jungle.

One night, over a gin, Kingsley inspired me to action with a statement that showed he could still influence my life with his words, just as much now as an adult as when I was a child: 'As an older man, one travels hoping that adventures will peel away the years. It is a shame when instead they peel the shutters from your eyes and add the years you denied you have lived already.'

The next day I awoke early and by mid-afternoon we had reached the sounds of a nesting ground. Although the trek had told on all of us, even our gentlemen companions had a younger glint to their eyes. It was a stirring sight., and you forget that the living animal before you is doomed to become the inanimate beauty that is the trophy on your study wall. Sitting there, guns ready, watching the Jub Jub in the canopy above, Kent and I actually began to discuss the differences in plumage and size. I even had time, for once, to sketch from life rather than from memory.

We burned Jub Jub feathers almost constantly in several small fires around the site – a precautionary measure I set up early but impressed upon the Indians to keep. The strange thing with burning feathers is the smell stays in your nose long after the fires stop.

Newton was funding the expedition and had realized that the extra days' travel had incurred extra costs. Although opposed to slaughter for plumage, he had no qualms with natural moult and instructed the Indians to stop burning and start packaging the feathers for cleaning and sale. More experienced guides would have continued to burn some feathers and package the rest; our less experienced guides just stopped burning.

Like the shadows of clouds, in their silence they came. Screams are often lost in the jungle amidst the cacophony sounds but a heavy man dropped through a canopy is unmistakable. I felt a fool as I threw aside my artistic renditions and grabbed for the instrument I am more skilled with.

Kent and I formed not only a thin but a short red line. Firing at the next wave of birds, we did little in the way of harm but at least managed to scare them higher.

I saw a sack so full of feathers that it looked like a Savoy pillow. I grabbed and threw it at the closest fire. There was an almighty explosion and the forest floor was soon ablaze as the oils caught and crackled. I summoned my two charges to me and soon we are running through the trees as best as an old man and a cripple could.

The birds were now almost a swarm as their nest site, too, began to burn. Kent's shout alerted me and I pushed Newton to the floor, as a Jub Jub with fantastic plumage flew inches above us and landed. It turned its sharp staring beak towards us and like a chicken struck at the ground as if we were grain.

I've had enough breached barrels to not trust a rifle after a fall, so I refrained from the obvious shot. Contenting myself with rolling the strangely inert Mr. Newton out of the way of the striking beak, I started to resemble the game of chance I have seen Russian sailors play with an outstretched hand and a sharp blade. I brought my hobnailed heel hard up into the underside of the beak and felt a sickening crunch. It didn't die but stumbled sideways, shaking its head like a befuddled prize-fighter.

I slowly stood before the monstrous beast, and watched as its eyes focused on me and let out that screech that plays havoc with the temperature of your blood. I drew and fired my back-up pistol right down the gullet and watched it crumple like a stake of cards.

Then I heard Kent's words echoing through the trees: 'Keep running, Jack. Remember they hunt in flocks.'

I did not speak to either of those men again after we returned to England, but I followed both their lives and their final glories. I will also say that I have only ever sketched from memory since.

Lambtons

I never claim to be a gentleman; I certainly refuse to call Kent my gentleman's gentleman. However, as an officer, I have been introduced to many gentlemen's pastimes, of which I find fly fishing to be the most relaxing. When I can, I like to take myself off to an idyllic spot and cast a few flies; it is always been less about the catch and more the scenery. There are few opportunities in my work to indulge this, unless you include the rare Lambton hunt.

Description

Primarily a deep-sea creature, the Lambton poses little threat to the Empire, unless one happens to end up in a trawl net.

The creature is about twelve to fourteen foot long with a snub nose full of small sharp teeth. Bony ridges run above its bright-yellow, lizard-like eyes and long barbells reach down from the front of the lower jaw, much like as in a catfish. The barbell length is fairly standard as a ratio to the body, allowing the creature to always stay just enough distance from the riverbed to compensate for its up-and-down undulating swim.

The Lambton does not have covered gills like a fish but instead has a series of nine gill holes like an eel. The Lambton has four stubby legs that are designed more like flukes to help with swimming, but it can also use them to walk along the riverbed at a fair speed.

The skin of the Lambton is brightly coloured, tending towards yellows and bright greens, broken up with heavy black irregular lines, one of nature's most obvious indications of poison. And indeed, its skin, which has the same texture as orange peel, contains a very potent toxin, making the creature fatal as a meal.

Every decade the Lambtons swim up the river Wear to spawn. The breeding process has taken place out at sea and it is the males who actually carry the young. Lambton spawn forms in blisters along the length of the male's body, Then, *en masse*, the Lambton swim upstream to the shallows of the Wear, where they roll around in the sharp gravel thereby bursting the blisters and releasing the spawn. Having done this, the males will return to the sea allowing the spawn to gain strength before they, too, return downriver.

The process sounds as if it might be fairly fatal as the creature would be covered in open wounds. However, Lambton skin has an amazing ability to heal itself – any break or cut just knits back together and the poison is so thick it acts as a strong adhesive. The males are weakened by the process nonetheless and go on a fairly devastating feeding frenzy on the return journey, practically emptying the Wear of fish. It is at this time the creatures show their ability to leave water for short periods, as they will also hunt down cattle and livestock in the fields bordering the river.

The Lambton has gone into local legend. Nature will occasionally play the Albion card and with the Lambtons it is no different. Most fishermen know to avoid the colourful creatures, but an inexperienced fisherman caught a white-skinned abnormality and, upon realizing his mistake, discarded the creature into a well.

In that confined space the creature slowly polluted the water, making the water of the area first undrinkable and later fatal. As it grew and insects could no longer satisfy its hunger, it started to leave the well to eat.

A few farmers attacked the creature only to see its skin heal before their eyes, and eventually the local landowner was brought in to kill the beast.

Legend obviously exaggerates the size of the beast and the battles it fights, but such tales do, however, prove Lambtons have been in the area for many centuries.

Lambton

Fig. # 1

Fig # 2

TENTACLES KEEP WURM 2FT FROM BOTTOM of WATER ALLOWING ROOM FOR SWIMMING. IN LESS THAN 3FT of WATER WURM SLITHERS VISABLY ON WATER SURFACE

Fig #1 Lambton out of water, note undefined feet
Fig #2 Lambton Swimming

Habitat

Little is really known of the habitat of the Lambtons as they are a deep-sea creature, and are only really seen at spawning time. Chinese legends talk of river dragons of brilliant colours, so they may not be confined to the waters off England's east coast.

Threat

Although the spawning only happens every ten years, the threat to livestock and the livelihood of fishermen along the Wear is quite devastating. The added threat of Lambtons poisoning the drinking water could be catastrophic.

Hunting

As an adult, the Lambton is a fearsome predator and should be approached with as much care as you would a Queensland alligator. Although the beast has a powerful tail, it relies chiefly on its small sharp teeth to attack and will use its flexible body to wrap itself around its prey, whilst it places a series of vicious bites to the head and neck.

On land, a well-armed hunter has the advantage, but the chances of meeting one of the creatures on land are quite rare so any serious hunt needs to be taken to the river itself.

The moment water is involved rifles and guns become fairly pointless. A good whaler's harpoon is a must and, as luck would have it, only fifty miles south of the river is the whaling town of Whitby.

Good, thick, oiled-leather waders are essential. They keep you nice and dry, allowing a longer stand in the centre of the river. The leather is also good protection against more playful nips.

Because of the hunting style employed by the Lambtons, you can pursue them only on their way back to the sea, which is unfortunately when they are at their most aggressive and are looking to feed.

When a Lambton swims past, throw your tethered harpoon into the beast, trying to get as close behind the head as possible, then retreat whilst the beast thrashes about, using up its strength. The moment the thrashing dies down, wade back into the water and, with your foot, pin the creature to the riverbed and use a bishop or club. A couple of good hard raps will end its life; alternatively, remove its head with a sharp blade.

Drag the body and head (if separate) to the bank as soon as possible to avoid toxins in the water. It is best to place the corpses on a large oilskin to avoid contamination of the bank.

I have been recently informed that, in China, 'river dragons' are culled with hand bombs thrown into the water. This may not sound particularly sporting but does sound fun, although I cannot imagine it is good for the fish.

The spratlings can actually be caught with a rod and line, although this does seem a longwinded way of doing it. The spratlings will be present in the shallow water for a couple of weeks after the spawning, and locals can be gathered together to slowly walk up stream with a large net, driving the creatures into manageable groups. They can then be gathered up and placed in pales of salt; drying them out neutralizes their poisons.

Personal Account

Owing to the infrequent nature of the spawning, I have only been on two Lambton hunts in my lifetime. On the occasion I will here recount, I did not so much join in, as spectate.

We received a telegram informing us that the Lambtons had started to spawn and had been seen at the mouth of the Wear. Unfortunately I was full of a sickness I had picked up whilst in Egypt and the thought of wading around waist deep in the cold waters of the Wear did not appeal to me in the slightest. It was Kent who pointed out that I had promised to take John Clayton on the hunt, the next time one chanced by.

Seeing as his soon-to-be lordship was about to be departing on his long-planned world tour, I realized this might be the only opportunity to keep my promise. We packed quickly, sent a telegram to John to meet us in Durham and left on the first available train.

John was a strapping lad and years running his father's estate had given him a thirst for adventure, outstripping that offered by the local landscape. Therefore the gentleman we met at Durham station was very excitable indeed.

On arriving in Durham we arranged transport on one of the carts belonging to the company building, the new Weardale Valley railway and journeyed to Wearhead, where the Lambton gathered in great numbers to release their young.

TIPS

The poison causes a rash when it comes
into contact with skin but this can be
eased with a gentle salt-water bath.

Gloves should be worn at all times
and butcher's chainmail gloves can
avoid the loss of a finger or two.

John told us of all his plans for his global tour as we travelled,
and I gave him advice on places to visit.

We set up by Wearhead Bridge, which had definitely seen better days. Local children were interested in our presence but their
better-informed mothers quickly ushered them away, only to
be replaced with some local men who set up a little posse on the
bridge to watch the fun.

I sat on the bank and draped out an oilskin on the exposed
gravel by the river. I placed my hunting rifle beside me, as well as
some bottles of gin and a selection of snacks.

I ignored the jokes from the bridge about picnics and the fact
that the 'wyrms' don't make good eating. Clayton and Kent,
dressed in their leather waders, tied off harpoons and waded out
into the fairly fast-flowing river. Their excitement was tangible
and I could hear Kent giving fairly pointless advice. As he was
today's designated expert, I chose not to contradict him.

I noted a few spratlings were already in the water and realized
that some of the adult males must have been and gone. However,
I noted some of the men on the bridge pointing upstream, and
following their gestures I saw the occasional colourful back of a
Lambton breaking the surface of the water as it came downriver
towards us.

I could see that Clayton was more than likely to be at the

receiving end of this beauty, so I shouted to him and warned him of its approach. He swiftly took up a magnificent pose with his harpoon that would have had him worshipped by most of the Shaka Zulu tribe instantly. If only his timing had been as perfect as his stance. He let his harpoon soar far too early and managed only to spur the creature on. I saw Kent taking aim, but shouted for them both to hold and let it go. Heaven forbid if my batman were to skewer a future lord!

It seemed the adventure had got the better of Clayton, however, and as the beast passed he drew his hunting knife and launched himself onto its back. In seconds the two were rolling about in the clear Pennine waters, Clayton's knife stabbing down repeatedly. I was on my feet, rifle in hand, but couldn't get a clear shot; the struggle seemed to last a decade but soon, with beaming smile, Clayton stood up, with the lifeless beast draped across his arms. The applause from the bridge was heartfelt and our peer-to-be grinned from ear to ear.

After several hours' hunting, we had three Lambton piled on the oilskin. I was feeling relaxed and rather enjoying the sunshine. A local lass had brought me a refreshing beer, pleasantly hoppy; the beer not the girl.

I positively jumped at the sudden appearance of a 'wyrm' right beside me. It had actually crawled across the land, and was probably looking for food, drawn over by the bodies of its fallen fellows. Its barbells briefly traced across my outstretched leg, tasting as they went.

The rifle didn't seem particularly sporting, after the excitement of Clayton's kill, but it served its purpose, allowing me to add my own trophy to the other three.

As the light faded we waited for a lift back to Durham. At the local public house, Clayton was very much applauded for his exploits, and I organized the local men to carry out a roundup of the spratlings in the next couple of days, promising them a couple of pennies for each one caught.

There were three very happy men on that railway carriage back to London, and as we left him at Kings Cross, we wished Clayton a safe journey. Little did we know that Lord Clayton would unfortunately be lost at sea during his grand tour, along with his wife and new-born son. I shall always remember him rolling around in the waters of the Wear, knife in hand. He will be much missed.

Lycanthropes

Many people have a beast inside them, but there are an unfortunate growing number where that beast is not just metaphysical but literal.

It is strange that in this guide to hunting Monsters I really did not want to include actual beasts. The lycanthrope is a beast inside the skin of a man but it is still just a beast. I fear for this reason they may pose the biggest threat to mankind.

Description

The Lycanthrope is like any man or women on the outside – never tending towards fat, but always having a lean athletic body. Hair is possibly coarser than that of a normal civilized human and can be unkempt and darker in colour. Hair is also more abundant on the body, causing eyebrows to be bushier or even join together across the forehead. The forearms and backs of hands often have obvious signs of increased hair growth. Skin has a brown tint at all times even in colder climates, and appears smoother, blemish-free and supple like that of a child or baby.

Just beneath the skin lies the beast. If the skin is cut, then soft fur can clearly be seen matted into the wound.

The word 'wolf' is bandied about with gay abandon. This image, however, comes from the Lycanthrope's home in the Germanic forests where they once mainly dwelt. This is a region where wolves were the beast to be feared. They took livestock, hunted in packs and, during the harsh winters when food was scarce and hunger ate away the natural fear of mankind, would kill the unwary. If the wolf is what you fear then the Lycanthrope may as well be a wolf. It is revealing that the only story I heard from India of a Lycanthrope cast the creature as a tiger.

For myself, I have hunted many of these beasts but never once could I truly compare one to any recognizable animal. I would go as far as to say that the legends of demons sprang more readily to mind in every encounter.

The Lycanthrope stands on its hind legs and walks like a man, but they are as at home on all four limbs, sprinting in a sideways gait that resembles the charge exhibited by mountain gorillas. Standing like a man the average Lycanthrope is close on seven foot tall. The body actually has a humped or arched back, positioning the head lower on the torso.

The powerful forelimbs are muscular and sinewy and longer than the arms of a man. Even the hands seem stretched and elongated, ending in thick stubby claws. The hindlimbs are like those of a wolfhound and give the impression of a man with long feet walking on his toes. These are shorter than the forelimbs and, when down and running as a quadruped, the beast has an upward slope to its body; it is again at this angle that the low-slung head shows itself to be a fantastic design of evolution.

The body appears fairly squat and powerful in comparison to the long limbs, fairly sparse of hair except for a coarse stiff mane that runs the length of the back, right up to the hump that is covered in a thick fur.

The head is bull-like, yet with a long muzzle with large canine teeth that jut messily about. The tongue is black in colour and lolls heavily out of the mouth. The eyes are yellow, each with a black pupil that seems to dilate sporadically and independently of each other, but alarmingly taking on human guise for brief moments.

I would like to say that the full moon is an old wives' tale, but it is a cold fact, that just like the tides, the lycanthropic change is influenced by the celestial body. This means you will encounter the beast only on the nights of the fuller moons – beware, it need

Lycanthrope

Fig #1

Fig #3

Fig #2

Fig #1 Detail of head
Fig #2 Quadroped stance of full figure
Fig #3 Track marks

not be completely full, just close, and the moon does not need to be visible.

Lycanthropes can hunt alaone or in packs and in beast form are violent and hungry predators. They do not kill for food but instead to quiet a bloodlust within. A beast on full rampage will do much damage in one night, shredding anything living they comes across.

The Lycanthrope is in permanent flux, its body seeming to renew itself the whole time, as it forever hovers twixt man and beast. This means that any damage done is soon healed and I have seen spent bullets actually pushed from the flesh to fall harmlessly to the ground.

The moment of full-blown transformation is an impressive thing to watch and I recommend the experience to anyone with the courage and stomach to watch. The eyes change first, sometimes up to an hour before the transformation. Then the body starts to sprout hair, the spine to rip and bend, and the mouth to fill with face-disfiguring canine teeth.

Finally the body seems to turn in on itself, accompanied by a nightmarish tearing sound that is hair-raising. Nothing is wasted and nothing is left behind. The whole process – apart from the initial transformation of the eyes – lasts about five minutes.

The strength, stamina and agility of the Lycanthrope form is beyond human, and that which would cause a man to stop in his tracks often is but a mild inconvenience to the Lycanthrope.

Habitat

As I have noted, the Lycanthropes can trace their lineage back to the primeval forests of Germany and their numbers have certainly increased around this area over time. Rumours talk of whole villages being given over to the sickness of Lycanthropy. Instances crop up all over the globe but an instinct seems to keep them near large forested regions. The man in them wants to be near people but the beast needs the wilderness.

Threat

Despite popular belief, the Lycanthrope does not pass on its malady from a bite or scratch. The real threat comes from the undisputable fact that the Lycanthrope is a violent and virtually unstoppable force.

A Lycanthrope in human form has the same potential for mating with another human as anyone. Successful mating between two Lycanthropes will always sire an offspring with the malady, and even with only one lycanthropic partner there is a good chance for the malady to be passed on.

Hunting

The beasts are so solidly built that it takes a hard blow to do any real damage to them; and where any damage is done it is likely to heal before the huntsman's eyes. It takes a sustained and persistent attack to kill the Lycanthrope in beast form, and the creature will never be scared away.

A mad and frenzied attack is all that can be expected if you engage or are engaged by the beasts. Alone, they are frightening enough, but in a pack you may as well find a good strong place to hide and let hope be your only weapon, for a Lycanthrope has both the sense and hearing of the beast.

The pack is only as effective, however, as the individuals within it. The pack can easily turn on itself, thereby giving you valuable time to escape their attentions.

If you decide to hunt Lycanthropes in beast form, then there are many good ways to do so. First of all, certain materials halt their healing process. Mistletoe, rye and recently silver have been found to have this effect. Wooden stakes freshly hewn, hardened, and soaked in mistletoe and rye make good fillers to pit traps; the same mixture can be spread on a blade.

Silver is a soft metal and whoever decided to use it against a Lycanthrope for the first time is a braver man than I. It is, however, a potent force against the Lycanthrope. Bullets cast from silver are possibly your best use of the metal's properties, as a blade, although more handy, is fragile and easily broken. I actually favour a silver spike mounted on the back of my forearm, which is so much easier to defend yourself with when in close combat, since a punch delivers a targeted blow better than a slash.

Lycanthropes have a couple of unique flaws, too. They eventually run out of energy. Admittedly, they do have what seems like boundless amounts, but in their beastly form this is burning out the entire time. If you put the creature through what would be considered a vigorous exercise, then sooner or later they will collapse and take on human form.

The easiest way to achieve this is by using a strong net. First take a net of good weave and condition and then soak it in a rye and mistletoe solution for several days before drying it out in the sun. This net is then harsh and repellent to the Lycanthrope and, once entangled, it will fight, hopefully in vain, to break free. The exertion will use up its energy reserve and leave you with an unconscious Lycanthrope in human form, vulnerable to your standard forms of dispatch.

The best way, however, to rid the world of Lycanthropes is to find them through detective work and capture them at a time away from the full moon. Open a wound to check for fur beneath the skin and then dispose or denounce, however you see fit. Many men and women have been tried in the courts and secretly hung for Lycanthropy.

Personal Account

I was in a party of six men on horseback; all of us were of British or German stock but no names had been shared as we were truly on a mission for our respective countries. We were riding along the river Neckar just outside Eberbach and the night was drawing in. We had built many traps around the area and every horse and rider seemed to be bristling with weaponry and nets.

Exhaustive investigation over many years had failed to turn up the human identities of two Lycanthropes in the area. Three hunts on the nights of the full moon had resulted only in tragedy and loss of life. Tonight we were set up for a fourth hunt and nerves were high. Secrecy had been great and now on a tip-off from our group we were approaching a painted Romany caravan. If our source was correct, our quarry lay within, for with the approach of every full moon this caravan always broke away from its fellow travellers and settled somewhere in the Odenwald mountains.

We approached the caravan at dusk and were surprised to find no horse or signs of life around it. One of the German riders, a gruff, heavily bearded man, dismounted, approached the doorway and disappeared inside; he emerged seconds later with a slow shake of his head.

The howl came from the wood and instantly every one of us had a rifle in our hands. The first brute burst from the treeline; he had emerged at speed on all fours and in the open he quickened his pace further, leaping for the steps of the caravan. The bearded man disappeared in a cry and a spray of blood and five rifles shattered the brightly coloured wood around the door.

I heard a cry beside me and turned to see a rider and his stead go down beneath the frantic claws of the second Lycanthrope. My horse luckily gave flight and took me speedily away from the angry creatures. All hell was breaking loose and I was already aware that this could be our fourth failed attempt; I had to seriously steady my nerves to bring myself to halt my bolting ride.

TIPS

Know your terrain — if you are hunting
a Lycanthrope in beast form then you
will be in dark forested areas at night.

Try to set traps — drop nets and pit traps work
best. Have a secure bolthole to retire to.

Wash well before leaving on the hunt and keep
your actions to a minimum to avoid sweating.

Never hunt Lycanthropes on your own.

Be aware that what you are hunting could have
a vengeful family waiting in the wings. Do not
walk into a nearby village boasting of your kill!

The horse stopped long enough to allow a dismount, but then
fled. I ran back to the group, which already seemed to be down to
just two men on horseback, somehow still managing to control the
panicked animals. I ran for the caravan and rushed inside, facing
the door with my rifle drawn. I saw one of the beasts stalk past
outside, shots tearing through its limbs causing gruesome wounds
that healed almost instantly.

It was a huge animal, barrel-chested and on all fours with an
impressive mane of hair that surrounded its head. It reared onto
its hind legs and I realized for the first time it was a female — the
Lycanthrope keeps many of its human traits. I aimed for her eye.
She had not paid any attention to me so far, so I had a few seconds
to get a good bead on my target and then fired.

My bullets were all silver-tipped and packed full of mistletoe
and rye. The female beast blew sideways with the impact and

stopped moving. At the same moment the caravan rolled over, as I heard the other beast slam into its side. There was the sound of splintering wood and I was covered in hot embers from the stove as well as other paraphernalia from the shelves and bed.

Pans bounced off my body and something sharp drew blood from my calf. I sat up and looked into the yellow eyes that bore down on me.

The Lycanthrope lunged forward, mouth agape, and I rammed my silver wrist spike directly into the beast's nose. It recoiled in agony and into a crossfire of shots that shook its body to a sudden stop. The eyes became human, then cold and dead, before the beast collapsed before me. I watched as the human form of a man, fragile and naked, reformed from the shattered remains of the fearsome beast.

I hobbled over the body and out into the cold night air. There, I am glad to say, I was greeted by the two remaining British huntsmen. We checked both beasts were truly dead, and buried the evidence, then torched the caravan and dead horses. We carried our deceased companions sadly home.

Manticores

The Great Game unfolded across the land of Persia, and as our Imperial swords crossed with those of the Russians, a beast that had long dwelt amongst the hills could not believe its luck that so much fresh prey had put itself within its reach.

Legend called it the Sphinx but we shall call it by its Persian name — the Manticore ('Man-Eater').

Description

Standing between the size of a big dog and a small horse, and on four strong feline legs, the Manticore is a majestic sight. Fur covers most of the beast's body and is tawny or golden in colour as well as short, allowing you to see the play of muscles beneath. Its most striking features, however, are the furless scorpion-like tail that springs from the flanks and the bunched wings on the shoulders.

The face, for it is truly that, has the broad features of the locals, until, that is, the creature yawns or gapes its mouth wide, showing the lion-like maw and impossible rows of teeth. The perfect killing machine.

Both males and females support manes but males have small horns hidden amongst the curls. Females carry their plentiful teats high on the torso so when sitting resemble the torso of a woman. This more likely serves as a lure to their chief prey — male humans — than as a biological necessity, although it does keep the full teats out of the dirt.

Their chief method of attack is by means of the scorpion-like tail; this holds a poison that does not kill instantly but does hold a punch of chemicals that disorients and prevents the blood from clotting. A sting from the tail and a single bite can be all that is needed. Weakened by blood loss, most prey will last less than an hour with very little extra effort required from the Manticore.

The wings are not for flight but merely serve as an easy way to cool down in the warm sun, by offering shade.

The Manticore is a strange creature — a solitary hunter by design, it is nonetheless not averse to hunting with others if the situation arises. This behaviour can mean that several beasts will roam in the same area, and surprisingly there is no tendency to territorial disputes.

The Manticore is purely carnivorous, only eating fresh meat, so is not prone to scavenging. They often do not leave carrion of their own either, preferring to eat their entire kill until they become bloated and sleepy.

The beast can lend itself to bursts of speed over short distances but is more likely to effect a feline saunter. The wings do allow a small amount of glide so the creatures are happy to drift lazily across the rocky terrain or can even pounce across exceptional distances.

The Manticore is far from a silent creature even when alone and has a huge repertoire of cries. Mewling, yapping, mumbling and barking seem to amuse these beasts and they almost appear to be talking; but it is a riddle what they are actually trying to communicate.

Habitat

Favouring open desert and the foothills of craggy mountains, and ranging all through the Old Persian Empire, the beasts can be found as far down as Egypt and even up into Russia. Although not territorial, the Manticore often has a favourite haunt and may make a cave or sheltered area its permanent home.

Manticore

Fig #2

Fig # 1

MAKES A
HUMBLE YAPPING
THAT SOUNDS
LIKE TALKING

Fig # 3

Fig#1 Manticore full body
Fig#2 The Manticore yawn,
destroys the look of the
human face
Fig#3 In watchful repose

Threat

The clue is in the name. The battlefields and marches of Persia
have an allure for the beasts, so keeping our soldiers safe is a must
if we are to keep our Middle Eastern ambitions alive.

Hunting

Apart from the wings and tail, the Manticore for all intents and purposes is a lion and should be treated thus in all but a few exceptions.

It is always best to hunt after the beast has already eaten its fill, as the Manticore will be less aggressive and agile as it will still be bloated and sleepy. Therefore, in hot areas, my advice is to set out early in the morning since the beast often hunts and feeds at night, when things are at their coolest. In more temperate climes, an early-afternoon hunt makes more sense, allowing you to catch the creature after its midday meal.

Unlike the lion, the beast cannot be lured to a spot with tasty meals whilst the hunter lies in wait – hanging deer or carrion from a tree will probably attract other beasts from the vicinity and most likely just flies. So a track-and-spot method is best.

To this aim, I recommend the use of dogs. Good hunting dogs will find a Manticore long before you do, worrying and flanking it, keeping it occupied until you can get a good shot. As with most beasts, a good rifle will penetrate the skull, but the males have particularly hard craniums so in most cases you will get a graze at most. Therefore it makes more sense to fire into the torso.

Native hunters of the Manticore prefer a spear, as one thrust can do a great deal more damage. A stuck spear can hamper a beast and, even if it remains unstuck, you do not have to waste time with a clumsy reload. Personally, I always favour a spear in Manticore hunts.

Manticore poison is not fatal to humans, except in very large doses. A full-grown man would need up to twenty strikes before he would possibly succumb to poison alone. The poison merely thins the blood and prevents clotting, and passes through the system in a day.

The initial injection has the feel of being hit by the bare-knuckle fighter Tom Paddock (I should know!), and the blow can even knock one out for a few seconds. The stinger is hard and thin so will penetrate most armours, so it is pointless to hamper yourself with bulky protective clothing. You should rely more on speed and agility.

Personal Account

So many times, over the years, I had been called to Afghanistan to run papers from one place to another. More often than not I ended up, during my visits, taking part in another Manticore hunt.

 TIPS

Always take plenty of fresh water and a smooth stone — Manticore hunts are often quite thirsty work and the Manticore often hunts away from water since it gets most of its liquids from its food. If you run out of water, place the stone beneath your tongue; your mouth will salivate and prevent the need for frequent drinks.

Don't be tempted to suck out or inhibit the flow of poison from a sting — the body deals with the threat easily after a good sleep. Try eating some salt beef soaked in black molasses to thicken your blood or drinking a few bottles of good stout.

If stung and wounded, try to keep your actions and therefore your blood loss to a minimum; bleeding out is exactly what the creature wants to happen. Even if you have killed the beast, you do not want to collapse from exhaustion and waste days in bed as you mend.

I cannot remember exactly why Kent wasn't with me this time but, seeing as the hunt was commissioned by a local military-run lodge, I went with a fellow named Peachy — a man full of big ideas and crazy schemes — two rather large, ridgeback hounds and a local guide. A reporter from the Pioneer newspaper was to follow us down the Grand Trunk Road — an Anglo-Indian schooled in England, he was as British as they come with a good understanding of the country and native traditions. Nonetheless, at first he was constantly asking questions about the hunt (he believed to be merely of the lion kind) and then questioning every answer.

If this? If that? I eventually told him to be a man and stop chattering like a society dame. After that we got on famously.

The hunt was to take place along the infamous Khyber Pass and we therefore dressed appropriately. The reporter and I favoured khakis for camouflage (something I am glad the military finally cottoned onto), while Peachy and our guide favoured the traditional dress of the area.

We packed a small case of Martini-Henrys but, as I have admitted, I much prefer the spear in moments like this, so, as we were riding, I had chosen a longer shaft for a bit of lance practice.

Our guide chose to walk, although he did lead a spare horse. I was slightly frustrated this would slow our progress, but it did make it easier for the dogs to keep pace without tiring and also for the less able riders to stay in their saddles on the rough terrain.

Peachy amused us for most of the journey with tall tales of his exploits and future plans. However, some became so far-fetched that we started to refer to him as 'Your Highness', a title he didn't take to, pointing out he was more a kingmaker than a king.

Our reporter fellow, on the other hand, was genuinely interesting in his comments on the landscape about us, and occasionally something he said would have you pause in your saddle to re-evaluate what you were actually seeing. For instance, on beholding the Khyber Pass, he stated that 'it was like a sword cut through the mountains'. I have never heard spoken a more apt description before or since.

I also became quite fond of the hounds on the trip and had taken to calling them Kent and Hastings, after my batman and mechanic back home. One morning, as we were packing up camp, 'Hastings' started acting up. This soon agitated 'Kent' and before we could stop them they were off into the low hills. Now you never follow a hound into terrain you are not familiar with; too many folks I know have gone after excitable hounds and got themselves into needless trouble. One friend of mother's, a Mr. Knight, had actually managed to fall down a well while chasing after his scatter-brained collie.

So we stood and watched the dogs go. The ridgeback is a brave animal and we could soon hear the barking of both dogs far up into the hills and then the guttural sounds of another animal. I felt myself physically wince when we heard the first yelp. I walked back to the horses, and took and loaded one of the rifles. Spear in hand (whose length I now regretted, since I was now on foot), I started off after the hounds.

Peachy and the guide followed on my heels. I am glad to say the reporter opted to stay with our things.

Climbing over the rocky, grassy terrain was much like trips to Snowdonia and I suddenly had a want for a nice glass of gin with some old army buddies like Thaddeus Tinker (who must be a major by now) or MacNutt, who did get so chilly in his regimental kilt.

The body of 'Kent' slammed down in front of us and took me from my thoughts. Just above us, though still partially obscured, the standoff between the Manticore and Hastings raged on.

I still don't know to this day why our guide rushed in. Maybe he was even fonder of the hounds than I. He stumbled as he reached the bluff and fell as if in prayer before the now visible beast. It was a female and judging by its teats had young nearby.

I realized that a hush had fallen for I could hear the strange mewling of the Manticore as it considered our guide. The guide raised his head, then in his own tongue said something. The beast seemed startled, its almost human face wrinkling with quizzical disgust, and then it struck with its tail. It all happened so fast that I did not even see the tail as it struck the guide, but I did bear witness as the unfortunate man toppled backwards off the bluff and down onto the rocks below.

The Manticore had the advantage of elevation and immediately turned on Peachy and me as we both recoiled backwards.

By some fluke of chance, the damn spear shaft, being so long, had lodged in rocks behind, holding me fast as the creature pounced, stretching its wings out wide. Its very weight drove the lance through its body, but it uttered not one sound as it perished there, in the lonely blood-soaked hills of the Khyber Pass.

'Hastings' was full of poison when we found her so I knew she wouldn't be long for this life and did the kind thing. Peachy and I then made our way into the higher hills and soon found the den and the beast's offspring. As pups, the tails are not yet fully formed and the nips are more playful than harmful, so at this stage were not a threat at all. Peachy emptied his sack of bedding and spare clothes and pushed the two pups inside, where they became quiet and still. I didn't question his motives; I knew from our talks it would be money or prestige he was after but I doubt they could have lived long in captivity.

On returning to camp we were surprised to find our guide alive, his head having been bandaged by our remarkable journalist. The two men became quite close friends on the way back.

I never could recall the reporter's name but the guide, it turns out, was called Gunga Din.

Martians

It is unlikely that any of you will ever experience the beauty of the Red Planet, stand on its alien surface and enjoy the feelings of health, freedom and power it brings. It is even more unlikely that you will encounter the parasites that have made that beautiful planet their home, alongside the indigenous species.

An anxious fear in my heart has made me include them nonetheless in this guide. I do not have a proper name for them, so have called them simply 'Martians', because, if they ever do come to Earth, that is where you will believe they have come from.

Description

The Martian has a body about the size of a brown bear and the shape of a pear stood on its narrow end. There is no covering of fat on the body and the entire thing is a mass of thick muscle covered in a skin that looks like oily seaweed. It balances and propels itself on a series of eight strong tentacles that sprout in a circle from the bottom of the pear-shaped body.

In the middle of the tentacles, and pointing towards the ground, is the creature's beak-like mouth which is segmented into three parts and made of a hard, almost ceramic-like material. About a foot above the tentacle mass is the creature's eyes, huge watery pools that are filled with evil intent. I have been told that shark's eyes speak of death, and, if that is the case, then the Martians' eyes scream it.

The function of the tentacles is not simply propulsion and balance; in fact, the Martian generally uses only three tentacles for such purposes. The rest of the tentacles serve as dexterous arms. One tentacle can be as prehensile as a human hand and a Martian can employ five such appendages at once. Fantastic speeds can also be reached when all eight tentacles are employed as legs, although the movement can seem like the creature is stumbling and spilling forward.

The body is huge but incredibly flexible, and can twist and turn in alarming fashion. At rest, the Martian will twist its body over, settling on the part of its anatomy which, at motion, would appear to be the crown of the head. In this position it can employ all tentacles as grasping limbs and will generally feed like this.

Martian society has similarities to ant or termite colonies, its members split up into workers, soldiers and breeders (I refuse to use the term 'queen' for these beasts), all with a slight difference in appearance. The workers have smaller eyes than its cohorts, almost completely black in colour and with three of their tentacles tipped with delicate jet-sharp crablike claws. The soldiers are as described but are the only members that can admit inky clouds that choke and disorient. The breeders – and there are many of these – are grossly bloated and give birth to live young that form in lesions on their bodies. The breeders' bodies crawl with earwig-like creatures that can only be the masculine half of this breeding cycle, as no other Martian seems to fertilize the breeder.

For fodder there are two main sources. First of these is their 'cattle' –a humanoid-like creature with delicate facial features, huge black almond eyes, and thin, weak bodies pallid in colour. Second is a cloying red weed that grows quickly and adds much needed vegetable matter to their diets.

The domiciles are huge communal domes where all aspects of Martian life take place, including technologies that surpass many of those on Earth. It is noted also that huge amounts of time seem to be taken up with what appears to be the smelting of inanimate components and storing them in huge cylinders. This activity – to the human eye – almost appears as a form of fidgeting in which workers are engaged when not busy elsewhere.

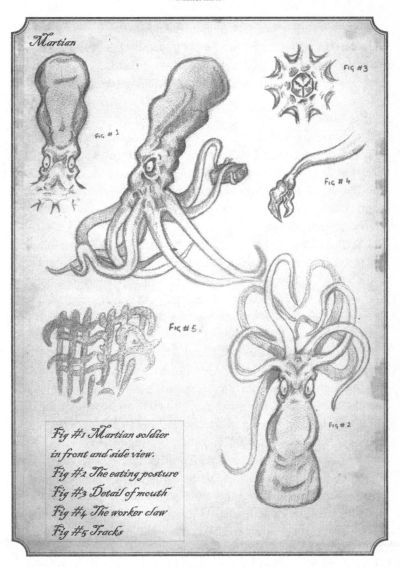

Martian

FIG # 1

FIG #3

FIG # 4

FIG # 5

FIG # 2

Fig #1 Martian soldier
in front and side view.
Fig #2 The eating posture
Fig #3 Detail of mouth
Fig #4 The worker claw
Fig #5 Tracks

Habitat

The areas of Mars which the Martians inhabit are always close
to the canals. As Mars has its own indigenous species, this brings
them into direct and open conflict, leaving the land around the
domes scarred by war.

Threat

Martians do not come from Mars. They looked on the Red Planet from their own dying roost and merely settled there. Mars is dying itself, so how long will it be before their jealous eyes turn our way?

Hunting

When you come across any normal beast, you have the advantage of superior intelligence. When you face a man, your intellects are matched; but when you face a Martian, you are the beast. Their intelligence is so far superior to ours that you seem but cattle to them. Remember though, you have 'horns', and even a cow can catch a farmer off guard.

Faced with a Martian, you need to stop thinking like a man but never forget you are human. Through history humans have over-come many predators, until finally, at least on Earth, we became the most successful species. Never forget that lineage.

Intelligence makes you arrogant and you start to believe you are indestructible. I have seen the best hunters taken down by their prey when this arrogance sets in. With this thought in mind, you must consider and learn from how animals hunt a superior foe. You need to hide and strike only the weakest each time, whittling down your foe until the strongest stands alone. Then you need to encir-cle or outflank this final opponent and only then take shots and deliver blows. If you can, escape and hide at any signs of danger.

The skin of the Martian is incredibly tough and the muscle structure beneath is solid, so small-calibre rounds and blades do very little damage. Shotguns loaded with solid shot penetrate well, as do elephant guns. Flame or concentrated heat work exception-ally well, as the skin and muscle of the Martian is incredibly oily in content. The natives' ray gun is possibly the best deliverer of such intense and controlled heat.

All the organs that support life are located in the thick end of the body and, as there is no bone structure present at all in Martians, these organs are particularly vulnerable.

Martians have no blind spot as their side-mounted eyes give it all-round vision, so to sneak up on one you need to find cover.

Each caste of Martian has a unique form of defence. In the case of the workers, you need to watch out for their crablike claws, primarily used for cutting through metal and other materials they use for building. A human finger or hands can easily be removed by these claws so extreme caution needs to be employed.

The Martian soldier is larger and the tentacles are stronger; it can also employ a sort of thick, black, ink-like cloud that impairs your senses. Although not fatal, it does cause nausea and headaches, and prolonged exposure can cause blindness. The indigenous species have developed a kind of 'face mask' that keeps the gas from the eyes and mouth.

Breeders are the weakest Martian form but defend themselves using the liquid they excrete to make nests for their new-borns. This starts off like water but quickly hardens into a tough clay. In extreme danger the breeder will coat any attacker in this liquid, rendering them unable to move.

Personal Account

The Mars campaign had already lasted a few years. Trade had been set up secretly between our two planets, and the British Empire had a military attachment at the disposal of the indigenous people (who did not refer to their home as Mars but instead have a name in their own tongue).

This was my only opportunity to prove my military credentials were worth more than the paper they were issued on. I was the commanding officer on board Her Majesty's Airship *M101* and had at my side my batman Kent and a crew of able airmen and soldiers. Mars had tested our metal against many of its hazards and we had already had run-ins with the Martians (as previously stated, not the name the indigenous people take).

On this particular day we were engaged in a standard watch on the *M101*, hovering just above the planet's ruddy surface. Every member was in full uniform and suffering from all the heat and discomfort that that brings. Kent was outside on the viewing platform, no doubt taking advantage of the cooling Martian winds; he was never an enthusiast for uniform. It was therefore Kent who

TIPS

Mars is a hot planet so light clothing is
recommended. If more daring or confident,
try wearing the garb of the planet's natives.

Mars has a lower gravity, so that on the planet's
surface your strength and agility will improve
and your stamina is under less strain. However,
this takes some time to get used to and a period
of adjustment is also needed on a return to Earth.

Know your Martian castes, as
each is different to hunt.

---

spotted the movement out in the valley.

Telescopes were brought to bear and it was soon identified as
a contingent of Martians. Six subjects were identified, and from
their sizes a guess was made at two soldiers and four workers. The
presence of the soldier type put the airship at risk, so myself, Kent
and four infantry men abseiled to the ground and set off at a yomp
towards the Martians, our native ray guns at the ready.

The valley area which the Martian group was about to enter was
overshadowed by dunes and coarse red brush. We split into two
equal squads and I sat and watched in our dune as three good men
ran across the open valley to the other side.

The heat of the blast was so intense it filled the air before us with
bright white light; a fizzing sound was followed by a large bang, as
the air itself fried. I could see falling ash through the spots in front
of my eyes and knew the team had been dispatched with ruthless
Martian efficiency. We were now trapped in the dunes, outnum-
bered and alone. Maybe it was the shock or maybe it was instinct
but we became the animals we needed to be. Survival at any cost.

I pulled the shotgun from the holster on Kent's back and passed him my ray gun; he was now armed with two of these and you could see the confidence spread across his face. Private Sneddon was on his belly, his radium rifle trained on the valley floor.

The Martian soldiers entered the valley first, spilling forward on six limbs apiece. Both were grasping, in their two remaining tentacles, boxes that resembled camera obscuras. We all sat quietly, our breathing slowing. Sneddon traced the path of their movement with his rifle, his sights never leaving his chosen target.

Our red tunics blended in seamlessly with the terrain, rendering us virtually invisible. We watched the Martian soldiers pass by and soon the workers came into sight behind. We waited until they had passed, too, and then Kent slid down the bank on his belly, not scrambling to his feet until he was right behind the workers. He fired his ray guns simultaneously and the air in front of him blazed blue, as each shot tore a new cauterized hole through the flesh of the Martians. One went down, followed by the other, but Kent was already running into the far dunes.

The same white light that had turned our comrades to ashes arched into the location where he had stood but moments before, and as the blast retreated it left, sitting on the sands, a perfect concave disc of red glass several feet across. The corpse of one of the fallen workers, although not in the blast radius, was bubbling from the heat in the air and within seconds it had caught fire and burnt, sending up a dense cloud of jet-black soot.

The Martian soldiers had turned on their tentacles and, with their distinct war cry, now started to head up into the dunes. It was then that Private Sneddon fired. The box weapon he shot, with pinpoint accuracy, exploded on impact and the sand once again turned to shining glass. One of the soldiers seemed to have evaporated into thin air but the remaining soldier, undaunted by the fate of his comrade, turned towards our dunes and let out a blast of the white heat. It sizzled through the air, leaving its distinctive molten trail across the sand from the valley floor and right between Sneddon and myself. Both of us suffered from the blast: my arm received serious burns and my uniform sleeve charred, and Private Sneddon was scorched badly along his back, his tunic ruined. Neither of us moved; although the pain was fierce, we waited as the thick black smoke from the burning Martians filled the air below our position.

Then, in elegant symmetry, we acted as one. I jumped onto the glass slope and slid down, gaining speed and trying hard to keep my balance, as I readied my shotgun. The slope was hot and brittle and shattered in my wake. The dark clouds were almost ready to enfold me, when the remaining soldier spilled out of the gloom, tentacles flailing. Sneddon's rifle crackled behind me and the Martian reeled back, a smoking hole in its upper body.

Blind from the cloying smoke, I slid to a halt in the soft sand. Through the inky blackness I made out a circular glow and fired both barrels in its direction. I heard the heavy thump, and shuddered as lifeless tentacles coiled out of the dark towards me.

When the smoke finally cleared, the three of us stood amongst the carnage. Sneddon held the surviving captive device that was miraculously still in one piece.

Kent used a signal mirror to call the airship and I stood and said a silent prayer over the spot of our fallen comrades.

Revenants

There are many versions of this particular Monster and the threat is present in all of us. The horror of my first encounter is still one that turns my stomach and sets my mind reeling. They are given many names, but the one that most chills the blood is the 'walking dead'.

Description

Perhaps it would be fair to say that a Revenant is simply a human corpse that does not seem to know of its own demise. However, there are a lot more subtleties to this phenomenon than just a dead person walking, and it is important to know of these so as to avoid mistakes and, more crucially, pointless deaths.

The true Revenant has colourless eyes, as a milky cataract forms over the lens after death. The eyes roll unfocusedly about, and seem to judder with every step; however, when focused on prey they become fixed, and on close inspection a black pinprick pupil can be seen at the centre. The mouth hangs open and the facial features appear slack, though the face becomes taut when the Revenant has targeted prey, the muscles tightening to allow biting.

Despite common misconceptions, it is unusual for a Revenant to be created from an attack on a living human. Like bears, the Revenant will usually go for the brain and other iron-rich organs of the body, and since the Revenant very much needs a brain and a working digestive system, this method of, let us say, procreation is not practical. For this reason, Revenants rarely show old bite wounds, as is often depicted in pictures, for once bitten a human is often devoured to a point that precludes reanimation.

A better form of identification is the skin. This quickly becomes yellowed and dry, often splitting and tearing to show the raw muscle tissue beneath. A Revenant will generally show a skeletal appearance, as muscle tissue and fat cells shrink. There will be a sinking and darkening around the eyes and, as time passes, ears, noses and lips rot away, hair and fingernails fall out, and teeth become brittle, breaking into jagged points and darkening in colour. Blood still flows but is more like a deep-red tar. Clothing may obscure other tell-tale signs such as a discoloured and hollow abdomen.

Revenants are prone to gluttony so will eat until they become bloated or even burst their intestines. They have no need for air so the chest does not rise and fall with the effort of breathing; they are therefore not hindered by airless environments.

Revenants usually move exceptionally slowly but deliberately, conserving damage to their muscle tissue. However, they can, if needed, make exceptional bursts of movement (in comparison to their normal sluggish speed). They can do this, however, only at the cost of muscle tissue and a spirited attack will leave most Revenants in a state of incapacity forever.

Revenants show a degree of intelligence, although of a basic and animalistic kind. They have no true social instincts left, although they cluster together in groups. When seen in a group, it can appear that it is purely by force of numbers they appear to overcome their prey, and not by a sense of tactics, but I can assure you: a lone Revenant is just as likely to overcome you as a concentrated group.

Revenants hunt mainly by sound and smell, only employing eyesight when close to prey. Therefore staying still and quiet is often the best means of evasion.

Habitat

Revenants feature in the folklores of many nations and therefore can be found across the world, with Revenant 'outbreaks' happening both in remote communities and in large towns and cities,

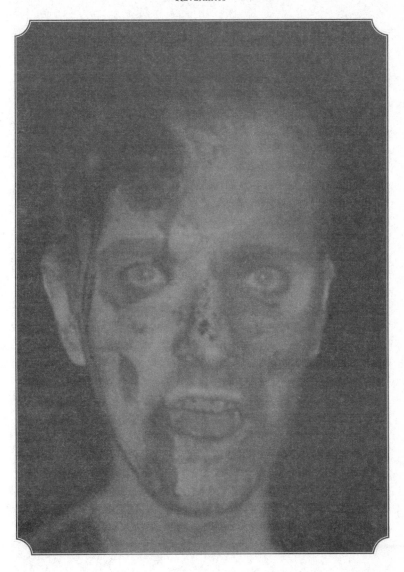

wherever, indeed, they can gain a foothold. Russia, India, Africa and Egypt seem to have the most outbreaks, but pockets have formed in the American South, the Pacific islands and right here in Scotland, Wales and even the streets of London.

The most famous outbreak in England was during the Black

Death; eventually the authorities carried out a controlled cull by means of a carefully planned fire in the City of London within whose walls the Revenants had been herded.

Threat

The threat and therefore the term 'Monster' applies to the Revenant by virtue of its disease which, if spread through the human race unchecked, has the potential to become a pandemic.

Revenant excretions of any kind get into the immune system very quickly. First, they act as a poison that kills the new host and then work to reanimate the body. Brain, digestive system, muscles and, to some extent, the heart, start to function again, while all other organs and pain sensors in the nervous system remain dead.

The fact that the Monster here is actually a *carrier* of a disease puts the Revenant in the same class as the plague-carrying rats. The actual carrier still needs to be exterminated but for a true end to this horror a *cure* must be found.

Hunting

Do not beat around the bush — go straight for the head. This is not hunting as art but hunting as brute force. Your aim is to knock out your opponent as quickly and as violently as possible. High-calibre easy-loading shotguns and bladed weapons are the order of the day here. Slow-moving targets that have no fear need a totally different style of hunting from that which you may already be used to. First and foremost, you yourself need to be completely fearless.

Revenants up close can suddenly change their pace to that of any human, so getting into close combat is not advisable. There are more pertinent reasons, too. A vigorous sabre slash may dispatch a Revenant before it comes into direct contact with yourself, but the spray of blood may get into your mouth or eyes and the virus will spread throughout your body. After an encounter, cleaning yourself and your weapons thoroughly of any gore is essential for stopping a later outbreak.

Personal Accounts
THE CASE OF THE WILLARD ESTATE

My first encounter with the Revenant was one of shock and surprise. I had heard talk of the walking dead; I had even heard the word 'Zombie' but nothing prepared me for the feeling you have when you are faced with your seeming fellow civilians who suddenly seem to have developed a craving for your soft, iron-rich insides.

The place was the Willard Valley, here in the green pastures of England. I was a dinner guest of Edward Thurlow and his wife, Samantha. There were other guests present at the house, too, mainly clergymen and other professional men. It had come to pass many times in my life that my services to the Empire had upset certain groups, often those who had a more arcane agenda than that of protecting the Realm and preserving the lives of their fellow human beings. Mr. Thurlow was one of these and it was with the aim of ridding himself of his enemies that he had invited us all to dinner.

We had only recently taken our seats to dine when Mr. Thurlow and his wife excused themselves on some personal matter. We continued to dine, then, amidst the fish course, the servants about us started to fall to the ground, struggling for breath. As quickly as they fell, they rose again and the real dinner began, so to speak.

Being brought up the way I have, I notice waiting staff more than most. When you see a face you have looked at alive come before you twisted and murderous with the distinct look of the dead about it, you feel your guts turn and you are far from able to act. My life would have ended right there, had not one of my dining companions, a doctor, put a hand in the way of a young maid's face.

The teeth sink into the flesh, and doctor's cry of pain brought my senses round and I was inspired to action. The fire, I had noticed earlier, had an ornate coat of arms above it and, under this, were crossed sabres. I pulled one from the wall and struck at the doctor's attacker with an inexpert aim, lodging the blade in the girl's skull. I turned back for the final blade and found a young man already grasping it, having taken my lead.

He plunged into the fray but within seconds I saw him fall. I snatched up the poker, scattering logs from the fire. Fifteen guests had sat around that table; five staff had waited on us; now only I stood alive watching the staff feast on the fallen guests. I backed to the window and when it resisted being opened I broke it with my poker and fled the scene.

Terror took me that night on legs like steel springs, but since then I have come to accept that I would have run whatever the circumstances; I could have saved no one in that room except myself.

Do not take me for a coward, for soon I returned with many men, and long before we came to the mansion we could see the fires and smell the smoke on the air. Edward and his wife were long gone and my tale fell on deaf ears. We watched the mansion burn, and the men and constables stood with me until the roof fell in. I do not know if anyone followed me out of that room but to this day I will not return to Willard Valley without a side arm and sabre.

The Case of the Infected Ship

The Queen had been in contact with Marie Laveau in New Orleans for many years, passing many messages back and forth. As a humble servant of the Empire, it was not my place to inquire further as to their contents. Mary unfortunately had recently passed away, and it came quickly to our attention that her host of servants might cause a problem if they had overheard any of the messages read aloud, so our Government decided to treat them all to a trip to England.

I have no idea what could have happened on board, but the ship was found adrift just off British waters and crammed with Revenants. You cannot just sink a ship like this, as Revenants can survive underwater. Having the undead walking ashore in Torquay would be just no good at all for the blossoming health and recreation industry down there, and besides which there may have been survivors.

Eight of us boarded the ship. We had plans to move from floor to floor, taking down any Revenant we encountered. I had reservations since I knew we would be unaware of cubby holes and other

Revenant

FIG # 1

Fig# 1 A member of the ships communication team
a Mr Ewen, sadly passed away as clearly seen here

hiding places and we would be facing Revenant in hand-to-hand
fighting, but Royal Marines will, in most cases, do anything they
are commanded to do at sea, and by this stage I was an officer of
some standing.

TIPS

Try to wear tough, hard-wearing clothing, especially if intending to engage in close combat. A chain mail vest, cuirass and gauntlets may seem like overkill but could make a crucial difference.

Try to wear goggles and a scarf over your mouth to avoid contamination. Stealth is paramount.

Never hunt alone — always have someone with you that you can outrun and are happy to leave as fodder for the Revenants.

Never get sentimental — Revenants look like humans of any age or gender; they may even look like friends. They are not.

On boarding the vessel, I was glad to say that we faced a mere handful of Revenants and I was proud to see the Marines act without emotion in dispatching them and with a high degree of skill and efficiency. I suggested setting up a thin red line on deck and making a noise until we had dispatched all the curious onlookers and this to some degree worked.

After a while, however, the Marines became restless and four of them set off to flush further Revenants out of the lower decks. On a fairly empty ship on a calm day gunfire can be heard with ease; it did not take a particularly morbid mind to realize four shots just didn't seem enough if the Marines had been successful. Night was falling and I recommended a return to our boat during the darker hours. A protest was raised about leaving comrades behind, and to avoid a potential lynching I reluctantly agreed a search for at least the bodies.

So four men, virtually back to back, descended into the bowels of the ship. It was on the lower decks that we found what the men later referred to, with admirable black humour, as the 'dining room'. Actually a large hold, it had become somewhat of a charnel house, where the Revenants still left on board were feasting on bodies of crew, passengers and now, unfortunately, Marines. The gunfire was deafening and instant, and I can only point out that a strong stomach is needed on a Revenant hunt.

It is not in a Marine's training to aim for the head. On deck, where no emotions had been in play, head shots had come thick and fast. Here in the dark and bloody 'dining room', with the thought of their fallen comrades blurring their good sense, they resorted to their basic and, in this situation, quite inappropriate training. Their volley of body shots were good at slowing the advance, but I must admit only I seemed to keep my head cool enough to aim my gun at the right level. I reloaded four times and can't remember a single shot not being a decisive blow.

I was distracted long enough for the three remaining soldiers to move forward to retrieve their fallen comrades and I paid scant attention as they pulled the bodies up on deck in the dark and onto the steam launch. We retired to the launch, satisfied no one was left moving on board the ship.

We took the launch around the ship, connecting explosives just below the water line. The whole process took just over two hours and by this stage we were working exclusively by lamp light. I remember the thump on the deck behind me and the sickening feeling of knowing my handgun was far from my reach; I had removed it earlier so it did not fall into the sea whilst I was setting explosives. The dead Marine was already clambering back up to his feet as I turned. His eyes were glazing over already and behind him shuffled his companions.

As I have said, any excretion causes infection and dragging your fallen comrades through a wash of Revenant blood was, I know now, ill-advised. From then on, they were doomed: bloodied hands had wiped hot brows, and tracks of now-contaminated sweat had worked into the eyes or mouths of the Marines.

I uttered a word I only use in the presence of sailors and soldiers and swung my fist hard into his face, holding his uniform front so he was unable to recoil. I followed this up with multiple blows until my hand throbbed with the pain of it all.

A launch is a small vessel, and if you position yourself right, with a person in front of you, then you are virtually untouchable. Eventually the Revenant before me was still, and being a good and well-equipped Marine he had remembered to pack a sabre as instructed. I drew it from its scabbard and, pushing his body overboard with my free hand, swung it in an arc as I did so, half severing the neck of the Revenant directly behind. I used the momentary pause that ensued to barge forward past the two remaining Revenant soldiers, and made it to my equipment belt with time to spin, aim and fire twice.

The explosion of the ship lit my way home, and by the time I reached port, my launch was scrubbed clean and smelling of ammonia. I likewise had undergone a scrubbing and I exchanged my clothes for the neatly pressed set I had brought from home for just this reason. I regretted the loss of my soft leather boots, however.

Shide

There is a lot of talk of the Shide, but it often does not sound like much to the untrained ear. The Shide are the creatures responsible for many of the legends of the fae, fairy folk, natural spirits and ghosts.

Description

So what exactly are the Shide and why would it be so difficult to spot one? The answer is simple: the Shide never come above ground (well, not anymore). They are buried and they dream, but the dreams of the Shide are not like the dreams of you and me – they take form.

The Shide themselves are tall, thin and elegant in appearance. Delicate features form their faces – large almond-shaped eyes, small noses, gentle, pleasing mouths and soft shell-like ears. Their hair and skin are translucent, reflecting sunlight in a way that gives them a radiant iridescence with a bluish glow. In dimmer light, you can almost see through the skin to the bone structure and internal organs beating and moving beneath. They do not wear clothes and seem to be in a trance-like state at all times. When they are first discovered in the soil they just look like corpses as the skin is dulled by the combined layers of dust and soil.

As you gaze upon them, you start to feel a pins-and-needles-like sensation inside your head, and then the dreams begin. The dreams can take on many forms but their nature seems dependent upon the age of the Shide. They can be incorporeal and ghost-like, small and secretive, or large and very solid. They are the legends of old and they exist to push you into fulfilling the goals of the Shide.

These goals might be classified as Luddite, wishing, as they do, to move mankind away from progress and industry. Sometimes Shide have been able to conjure enough dreams to stop a whole village from advancing out of the Dark Ages. And in areas where progress seems unstoppable, they can conjure creatures to sabotage, wreck and hinder.

Habitat

The Shide are more prevalent in the British Isles than anywhere else in the world, although they do also seem to inhabit swathes of Europe, and from stories I have heard even Russia, India and Japan.

Such areas tend to be backward or rural, where the old ways are more favoured than new. The locals may shun modern medicine and favour herbalists. Sites that have born witness to many witch trials in history often coincide closely with Shide activity. Long barrows also seem to point towards the presence of Shide.

Threat

Progress is the foundation stone of our Empire. Every day we see manufacture become easier and faster. Illness and mental sickness is being treated in more effective ways and there are huge advances in travel and education.

We must press swiftly onwards in protecting both our own shores and lands further afield from our enemies. Then, as our weapons become ever greater, we shall be able to turn our noble and imperial ambitions to the stars and the ocean's depths.

The Shide is the enemy to all progress and hence to Empire. I challenge any man to hold a dead child in their arms because of poverty, illness or war and not wish we were progressing faster.

Hunting

It is fortunate that the Shide leave markers to show their burial places. Fairy rings — a circle of fungi or discoloured grass where

Shide

Fig # 1

Fig # 2

Fig # 3

Fig #1 Detail of Shide head as perceived

Fig #2 Placement of fungi around buried body, appearing as fairy ring on surface

Fig #3 Shide dream as seen in Wood mill

fungi have once grown – give away the threat buried beneath. If you ask children, they will always excitedly tell you where fairy rings are located. However, never travel with them directly to the location, but wait until mid-morning, a time when you can look completely in keeping with the locals as you walk through the fields with a spade.

Dig up the fairy ring. You will possibly need to dig about six feet down, maybe further, as soil quickly gathers above these places and very little footfall wears them down.

Trust me: however deep you need to dig, you will eventually discover a sleeping Shide at the bottom. They will be curled tightly in a foetal position. The moment you have uncovered the Shide you have two choices, dependent on your sensibilities. You can dig it up and remove it from the lair and have it encased in iron to prevent dream leakage. The other way is to use an iron spade to do your initial digging, and then, on uncovering the Shide, make a simple clean blow to the neck to sever the head. Thereafter the body only needs to be buried again. However, it is never as easy as that, especially if you go about the task unprepared.

To protect yourself from the Shide's dreams, you should wear iron plates across your head. An iron-lined bowler is ideal. This will also serve to prevent the Shide from reading your intentions in advance and sending an advance party of dreams to derail you.

The dreams themselves, as I have stated, can come in all shapes and sizes but they are all formed from the same stuff, against which cold iron blades are the best form of attack, although any weapon will harm.

There is a strange form of defence against the dreams, in the shape of stone amulets with naturally occurring holes through their middles. Carrying one of these renders you undetectable to the dream creatures, though the reason for this is not yet known. The same talisman, however, does not work against the Shide themselves.

Personal Account

We had taken it upon ourselves to check out a saw mill that had been closed down owing to constant malfunctions. We had heard rumours from former workers about creatures living in the machinery but in reality I think we thought we were having a pleasant jaunt to the country.

After talking with the mill owner we started to get the feeling

that his mill had been overrun with nothing more than the usual destructive vermin and not some new kind of creature that needed to be investigated. So we took our ratting rifles and went to do the owner a favour.

The mill was huge, and heavy machinery sat unmoving amongst the dust and detritus. We unslung our rifles and started to poke around but we saw no signs at all of rodents. Kent threw a lever and the gears ground into life, turning a large material belt which filled

TIPS

Remember cold iron is a fantastic
defence against the Shide.

Shide often manage to build up good follow-
ings amongst the locals; do not ask too many
questions in the villages that might lead people
to suspect your intentions and betray you.

Dreams are all different but regional
similarities tend to occur and can lead to a
distinctive local folklore over the centuries.

---

the air with sawdust. That is when *they* swarmed out of the rafters.

They looked like a cross between tiny monkeys, dragonflies and frogs, and they tore into the material belt with relish. I looked at Kent and laughed as I took aim.

There were about sixteen of the critters, and after our initial shots, the others took to the air again, waiting for us to chase around after them and pick them off. Pretty quickly we had them all laid out on the wooden floor like grouse after a day's shooting. It was only then that my mind started to go down the right route and I realized these were Shide dreams.

We went up to the top floor of the mill and looked out of the tall windows onto the surrounding landscape. Behind the mill was an empty stable yard and, although the sparse ground had been churned up by its previous occupants, you could still make out a fairy ring. It was partially within the grounds but a large section also seemed to disappear beneath the flagstones.

Kent and I worked into the late afternoon, levering up flagstones and digging down into the soft rich earth. I felt the tingle, as did Kent, but we didn't have the right stuff on us, so we just dug faster singing old army tunes to make our minds more difficult to read.

By working hard we soon managed to uncover the Shide. It is difficult to explain just how perfect and beautiful these creatures are and I can fully understand why some people have stowed them away in iron coffins rather than destroying them. We had both gone quiet, looking down at the perfect naked female form before us, the tingle in our brains intensifying all the while. Then the sun was obscured by clouds and we saw the inner workings of this creature, and just for a few seconds it was no glamorous goddess before me but a beast and my shovel came down with speed.

A moment later I felt Kent lunge forward and I had to block the swing of his shovel en route for my head with my forearm. It hurt like hell as my bone took the full force of the heavy wood without breaking. I swung my fist into his jaw, taking my friend clean off his feet and onto the uneven floor of the pit.

I saw his eyes clear and we said nothing as we crawled out and refilled the pit in silence. James wasn't the first man I had seen overtaken by the glamour and he won't be the last.

On a different note, I had a gun cabinet made from wood hewn at that mill after it reopened just a few months later. I gave it as a gift to Kent.

Snark

The beauty of hunting lies more often than not in the small game hunts, where the quarry takes a measure of skill to track and kill but is less of a threat when encountered.

I have not as yet seen a fatality caused by a fox, but there have been very few Boxing Days in England when I have not failed to mount up and chase one around the countryside.

The same is true of the Snark; the hunt is still enjoyable and fun, even if it does pose a slightly bigger threat than a fox.

Description

The Snark is an odd-looking creature about the size of a pit bull terrier with a large colourful, almost snail-like shell on its back. A quadruped, it has a shuffling gait and a stocky body covered in feathery tufts of brownish fur. The four legs are stubby and end in three toes surmounted by thick, tough, curved claws used for digging up roots and breaking mussels off rocks.

Its head is set upon a fairly sturdy and yet flexible neck. The head seems at first to consist solely of rather large buck teeth, much like a rodent's but thicker. On closer inspection, set back from these teeth, are large rather expressive eyes with heavy markings, giving the Snark a serious look at all times. Beneath the eyes sprout small tusks right out of the flesh, used for levering mussels open.

The shell is splendidly and colourfully striped and its entire area is covered in small holes. When the Snark is safe inside this shell, small poisoned tipped spines push up through the holes. The spines are also striped and end in very sharp red ends.

The poison the Snark slowly excretes from these spines is highly toxic and does not mix or dilute with water, having the consistency of oil. This is a poison that causes instant vomiting and stomach cramps, seizures and eventually death. Although it oozes only whilst the spines are extended, the dripping oil-like substances slowly covers the shell in a waxy 'varnish' that dries and cracks, making the shell resemble the peeling paint as seen on bathing huts popular along the Margate coast.

The Snark will walk along snuffling the ground for hidden roots, and the sound can often be heard long before the creature itself is spotted.

If attacked or cornered, the Snark will protect itself by biting. Its strong teeth can easily remove flesh or fingers and they can rear up to use the front digging claws to scratch and gouge. Never do they retreat to their shells and use the spines as a form of defensive attack, but be aware: poison can be present on their teeth or claws, a residue left from preening their shells, and will still be as lethal.

The Snark lives by rivers and coastlines, where their preferred food is available, and they have a peculiar sleeping habit of moving to the edge of the water and retiring into their shells. Coastal Snark can sometimes be completely submerged by high tides. However, they never seem to drown, suggesting air pockets form in the shells.

The Snark is a communal animal that gathers in little packs; it is possible to come across groups numbering almost thirty-strong. Amongst these groups, immature Snark are prevalent, since they are safer in larger numbers when their protective shells are still soft. The toxin is present but in a far weaker form.

The Snark lays clutches of eggs in hollows beneath tree roots. Young Snark will remain under the tree for several days after hatching, eating the roots. This means that the adult Snark do not return to a clutch of eggs and often predators dig up and eat the young.

It has been noted however that a large clutch of eggs left

The Snark

Fig #1

Fig #2

Fig #3

Fig #4

Fig # 5

Fig #6

Fig #1 The Snark
Fig #2 Position in shell
with spines deployed
Fig #3 Tracks
Fig #4 Spoor
Fig #5 Skull showing teeth alignment
Fig #6 Egg cluster

undisturbed and resulting in a good-size brood can often be the downfall of a tree, as the root system is completely undermined and destroyed.

The Snark is an extremely lazy animal, possibly due to the excellent protection it enjoys whilst asleep; this results in the creatures often sleeping for days on end.

Habitat

The Snark can be found in many different locations but will favour rocky coastlines where shellfish cling to the rocks or freshwater rivers where hardy trees, tubers or vegetation grow. They prefer temperate climates to tropical or arctic ones.

Threat

The Snark becomes a threat by accidentally poisoning waterways. Its potent oily poison and habit of living around water makes it a foregone conclusion that if you have Snark you have spoilt water. Coastal Snark, living just below tidal waters, are more often than not placed exactly where sailors beaching landing craft will step. In fact, the mere presence of Snark on an island makes it uninhabitable.

Hunting

Although brightly coloured, noisy and living in sizable packs, the Snark is possibly one of the most elusive of prey and it takes really good and polished knowledge of tracking before you will even be able to engage in any kind of hunt.

Snark are never far away from fast-flowing waterways so if you do not have the sea, stream or river in sight then you will certainly not find a Snark.

Once you have found your waterway, the next step is to check for a food source. By the sea, you will first be looking for mussel beds; these will always be beneath the high-tide mark on rocky outcrops and Snark activity will be obvious owing to the large piles of spoil, shattered shells and heavy scratch marks on the rocks where the muscles were once anchored.

The best time to look for signs of Snark activity is as the tide is on the turn and making its way back in. This allows time for the Snark to have foraged without the evidence being washed away by the tides. In the case of inland waterways evidence of foraging for roots and tubers will be harder to spot – the soil is dug with the front claws and the Snark has a habit of then walking over its dig, thereby covering its own tracks. The best sign to look out for are roots that are slightly proud of the ground and have been chewed

to the moist core with only the drier husk left.

Once you have established the location of feeding sites, it is then a case of stalking backwards and forwards along the length of the site usually taking in an area of around half a mile to a mile. Eventually you will come across a Snark, either sleeping soundly beneath its shell or still engaged in foraging.

Funnily enough, the final part of Snark hunting is a simple act that requires only a few specialized tools. Thick leather gloves with metal fingertips, a long-handled two-pronged fork, a broad-bladed double-edged knife or dirk, plus plenty of care and a little hope.

A sleeping Snark should be approached quietly and flipped, then stabbed through the soft underbelly. A Snark in defensive mode should, however, be approached with a great deal more care. The head moves easily on a strong flexible neck and the bite is often poison-coated. They will move on their hind legs so they can scratch and gouge with digging fore claws.

This is where your fork comes in. In adopting an aggressive stance, the Snark will rear onto its back legs, However, it is a quad-ruped, so with a little patience (and a bit of distance) on your side,

TIPS

Patience is a virtue, remember the Snark is not a
predator, so biding your time can usually lead to a
perfect hunt.

Wear thick-soled boots as a shed spine or concealed
sleeping Snark can be trodden on.

After handling a Snark, do not remove your gloves
by the popular teeth technique — it will be the last
time you do it.

Beware of Boojams (see *Personal Account*)!

---

the Snark will eventually drop back to all fours. This is when you
leap forward and pin the Snark by its neck to the ground. Pinned
in this way, the Snark remains helpless and can be dispatched once
again with your blade.

Snark offer very little in the way of nourishment, and since
souvenirs must be vigorously scrubbed and cleansed before they
can be exhibited as trophies, usually the only satisfaction to be
gained from killing a Snark is to know you are removing a threat
to the Empire. In my opinion, once your hunt is over, the best
thing to do is dispose of the corpse on a bonfire. The good thing
is that the oil-like poison actually burns exceptionally well and
maintains an extreme heat.

Personal Account

I had been on another hunt and it had not gone as well as I had
hoped. Three men were dead and the organization was massively
below par. This meant the team was split, with myself leading a
group of three in the island interior. I should mention at this point

that one of our number was also suffering shock and a couple of broken ribs.

The other group was five in number and was waiting at the coast for our return; they were also about to have their second disaster since we had landed. They were sitting by an inland waterway that soon after joined the sea and were using it as drinking water to mix with their whisky, which apparently was imbibed to steady their nerves.

One of the hunting party started to vomit quite badly, became unconscious, and, despite intervention by the medically trained skipper, was soon dead. It was at this point my hunting party returned, just in time to witness another party member entering an unconscious state; he also died moments after.

I saw the tell-tale rainbow staining on the water's edge and instantly alerted the group not to continue drinking the water. Both men had died after using the same canteen so it was assumed for now this was the tainted source as no one else was ill.

Since we had landed on this island we had already lost three men to predators and, now with two more lost to poisoning, our numbers were dwindling fast. The party's organizer wanted us to return post-haste to the Scottish mainland, realizing that the death toll among so many prominent businessmen would raise difficulties. I, on the other hand, pointed out that the island had Snark and therefore it was our duty to hunt them down and dispel the threat, especially as the infected water was so close to a natural port. I of course won the day.

This time I set out into the island's interior with three other men — the hunt organizer, a clergyman who had been with my party, and a proprietor of one of London's finest meat markets.

We had the evidence of the polluted stream to show us that we need only walk its length to find our quarry, and we were rewarded within a few hours. Light was fast fading but we came across a pack of Snark already settled for slumber. I counted seventeen brightly coloured shells either side of the water, spines extended, leaking their toxins into the fast-flowing stream.

Before I could explain about the way to kill slumbering Snark, a rifle had retorted beside me and the closest shell exploded in a hail of spines and fragments. One brightly coloured piece embedded in my arm, and my face must have shown more fear than shock because the butcher was on me in a second.

He tore off my sleeve, dislodging the shard in the process, and used it as a tourniquet. The pain caused by the tightly bound material brought me to my senses and I gave the butcher free rein as he pulled out a large hunting knife from his sock, cut my arm deeply above and below the wound, and then squeezed the flesh, milking the blood from me.

Finally satisfied he had removed all trace of the toxin, he washed and bandaged my wound with more torn material. For now, he did not release the tourniquet, but told me to sit. Remarkably, the sleeping Snark remained so – despite the loss of one of their number they had not stirred an inch. I did as I was told and, having informed my companions of the correct way to kill Snark, watched as they went through the pack, flipping each shell with care and using blades to dispatch the Snark before they woke.

We set a funeral pyre there and then in the woods and burned all the Snark corpses, My tourniquet was removed but I still suffered a few hours of nausea, for even with the prompt care given by the butcher, I was still feeling the effects of the poison, albeit in a lesser way than our two dead companions.

We returned to the beach again when the sun was starting to rise. The tide was a long way out, leaving our boat stranded on the sand, so we took the time to collect our dead and bring them on board. The hunt organizer suddenly let out a whoop of joy that was quite out of keeping with the sombre situation, and set off along the beach.

We all watched and realized he was approaching a colourful Snark shell exposed by the retreating tide. We saw him flip it, knife ready, and then he let out several large yelps before returning at a limp, covered in fresh blood from wounds to his legs.

It would appear he had found the shell to be filled with a large form of aggressive hermit crab that had used its claws to take two rather large chunks out of our host's left knee. I have since found out that the Boojam (the crab in question) uses old Snark shells as its home. Immune to their poison itself, it relies partly on the residual poison on the discarded shell as protection, but failing that will snip at any interloper with its sharp claws. The Boojam, although painful, is not a threat to the Empire, only to the foolish and unwary.

Vampires

As I remember, I was sitting reading a copy of Bram Stoker's famous work and gently chuckling to myself. I was in the very hotel he had stayed in, and my room looked out over the very same valley that had inspired him to write his romantic drivel. I reminded myself it was just a fantastical story, gothic nonsense, and nothing to do with actual Vampires. If you really want to be scared, you need to meet the real thing.

Description

The initial impression given by the Vampire is of sickness: it is pale and drawn, with sunken eyes and jerky in movement. Teeth are generally peg-like, long and discoloured. Eyes are small and dark and hair (if present at all) is coarse and opaque. This, however, is the Vampire at its most dangerous, as this describes a Vampire that needs to feed.

The fed Vampire is easier to spot as they are obscenely bloated, their skin a mismatch of vibrant colours from deep ruddy reds to rich purples. The mouth is black and crusty scabs are thick around the eyes, nose and lips. The teeth seem shorter as the gums have become puffy around them. It is the smell, however, that really takes your breath away, a carnal house reek that generally renders most victims incapable of action, long before fear sets in.

The Vampire's movements now seem fluid as if every joint and limb is flowing on water. The bloated body moves with a sickening swaying action, as the vast amounts of blood slosh about inside like the tides. Veins criss-cross this whole ghastly apparition like a map of the canals of Mars and stand proud like steel cable. As horrific as the Vampire now looks, it is possibly the safest time to approach it.

Once bloated in this way, the Vampire will seek out soft earth and burrow down deep into the soil to hibernate. They can remain in this state for anything from a few weeks to a year, depending on weather conditions and the amount and quality of blood gorged upon.

Graveyards naturally offer a well-dug and rich soil and a Vampire rising up to feast can often give the impression of being a member of the recently departed returning from the grave. It is more likely, however, for a Vampire to go to ground in swamp or marshland.

Vampires are intelligent and cunning. Unmolested, their feeding cycle can go on for many generations, which has led to legends of immortality. Warm weather can use up their blood reserves quickly and result in a more frenzied and frequent feeding pattern, whereas cold winters (especially those resulting in a deep frost) can lead to a torpor that slows digestion, therefore increasing gaps between attacks.

Vampires are solitary creatures, needing a hunting ground that will support them alone, and therefore they are fiercely territorial against interlopers.

Vampires appear to breed only once in their lives and the act will nearly always result in two offspring, a male and female. The birth process seems to be the end of the mother, and the children do not emerge for the first time until they are fully grown and capable of the hunt.

Young females emerge with rudimentary wings which they use to carry them many miles away from their brothers. The wings remain sometimes, but in most cases are dislodged after their first hibernation.

Vampires feed by slashing open the throat or groin, either by tooth or nail, and then lapping or sucking the blood directly from the wound.

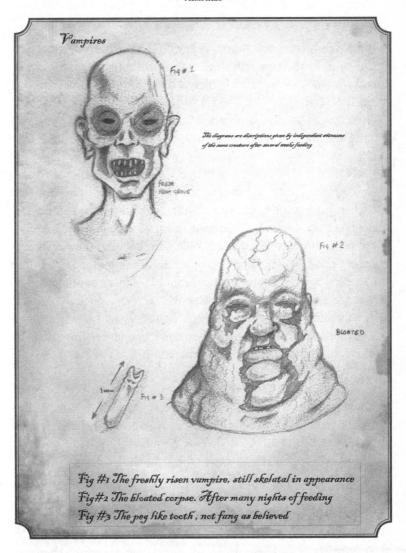

Vampires

Fig # 1

The diagrams are descriptions given by independent witnesses
of the same creature after several weeks feeding

FRESH
FROM GRAVE

Fig # 2

BLOATED

Fig # 3

Fig #1 The freshly risen vampire, still skeletal in appearance
Fig #2 The bloated corpse. After many nights of feeding
Fig #3 The peg like tooth, not fang as believed

Habitat

The Vampire has spread all over the globe, much like Man. They are especially common in isolated communities of a fair size, surrounded by swampland and frozen tundra. Necropolises or grandiose graveyards can be a likely dwelling place, making Paris, New Orleans and Russia favourite haunts.

Threat

Vampires only have one source of food – humans.

A Vampire will always kill its victims and a feeding spree will usually include around ten kills. Thus, a maximum of fifteen hunts a year gives a potential of one hundred and fifty kills. You do not need a lot of Vampires before a lot of humans begin to lose their lives.

Hunting

Vampires are easier to hunt in their dehydrated state and are sensitive to the saps of certain woods. Ash, hawthorn and oak all seem to bring about a violent reaction in the Vampire's blood reserves; if the blood becomes tainted in this way, they will eject and vent the blood as quick as possible. The blood spews either through open wounds or from an available orifice. In general, this makes for a fairly horrific spectacle.

If you are faced with a Vampire in its bloated state, a sharp wooden stake delivered to any part of the body will result in venting, but a stake to the heart or mouth will poison the blood supply more effectively.

Once a Vampire is dehydrated or devoid of blood, they become weaker and their movements are slower and jerkier. This is the perfect time to remove the beast's head. Vampires can go to ground and, with enough blood, can heal themselves fully, even growing back missing appendages, just as the salamander does. However, there is no recovery if the head is severed.

A better way to hunt the Vampire is to track down where they have gone to earth. Bloodhounds or pigs are particularly good at routing out a buried Vampire, especially when bloated. All that is then needed is a sharp spade for both digging and decapitation.

Personal Accounts

THE CASE OF LORD RUTHEN

I have spent more days than I care to mention thinking about Lord Ruthen. Of course I never actually got to know his real name; I just didn't like this encounter to just be between me and

some nameless beast, so I picked a name of my own.

Tales I had picked up around the slums of Paris led me to the catacombs beneath the city's streets, and I went down with just myself and a truffle pig I had borrowed for the occasion. I was armed quite simply, with a belt full of stakes and my sabre. You

TIPS

The Vampire will most often try to rend
the neck in a fight, so a gorget is a practical
if cumbersome item of additional clothing.

A face mask will keep blood out of the mouth
and nauseating smells out of the nose.

A steel spike has more piercing power than a
wooden stake, but gives far from the desired
effect ... unless you have the forethought to
cover the spike in the appropriate tree sap.

Bullets are not effective, as the body is less
dense than a human's. The damage caused
by even a large-calibre round is little, unless,
once again, the bullets is coated in tree sap.

Remember: some female Vampires may have
retained their wings — it can come as a shock
when they suddenly launch into the air.

Wear old clothes — by the end of a
Vampire hunt you will not want to
keep whatever you were wearing.

---

can really take it back to old school on a Vampire hunt and I had
become quite arrogant about my prowess against these Monsters.

I let the pig take the lead but very quickly realized that the
smell of Paris's medieval sewers was far too strong for her sensitive
nose, so I tied her up and went looking for signs on my own. I was

getting tired and had decided to head back, when I walked right into the Vampire I was hunting.

More than ready for a feed, the Vampire had skin that was almost translucent, so pale was he. I could see the shape of the muscles and bones beneath, and he smelt of earth and dust. He wore an elegant Parisian suit that had seen cleaner days.

The Vampire's first strike hit me across my face but I had the experience to go with it, allowing myself to be thrown through the air, rather than resisting it, and taking an impact that had enough power to render me unconscious or tear the skin from my face.

I landed well and rolled, springing to my feet and sprinting through a sluice gate, which I immediately slammed shut behind me. The Vampire jerked up to the gate and cut off my escape; I had inadvertently entered the bottom of a very deep storm drain with no scalable way up.

It was then that he spoke. He had a heavy East European accent but spoke fluent and lilting French. He explained almost poetically to me that I was to be his first kill in almost ten years and how he would savour the taste of my life as he drained me of my blood. He told me of the years he had walked the Earth and how my blood would merge with the blood of many Vampire hunters before me and allow him to walk the Earth for many more years to come.

Before he could say another word, however, my blade sank effortlessly into his throat and I watched his eyes lose all their arrogance. As I pushed the gate open, he stumbled off my blade. One downward slash and the body and head parted company.

It is moments like that whose memory I have grown to hate in my old age. Killing a Monster is a service to the Empire, but a Monster that talks is a man, and every time you remember that you also realize that, from the other point of view, you are the Monster.

The Hunt of the Bloated Corpse

I love New Orleans and see the French quarter as a second home. It was the birthplace of my mother, before she came to England and the London clubs to ply her trade, earning the money and respect that gave me the life and freedom I could be so proud of.

Every time I return to these streets I meet up with old acquaintances and together we go on into the swampland to hunt the strange and wonderful beasts that frequent this harsh and difficult terrain.

That particular day we set out without knowing what we would come across. Three days in and we came upon a village in which there was much wailing and gnashing of teeth. We quickly discovered a Vampire had been at work. In a village of around thirty people there had already been seven deaths.

After some initial questioning concerning the frequency of the attacks, we soon discovered that almost all of them had taken place during cray-fishing expeditions in a certain area of the swamps.

It did not take us long to gather a group together. There were two Creole guides from the village, myself, my friend (and stalwart batman) Kent and three of my hunting companions of old. We journeyed along the bayous in shallow-bottomed boats, until at last we reached the extensive crayfish fishing grounds. We set up camp and split into three hunting groups. Kent, a guide and myself made up one group, and we spent several days hunting amongst the odd-shaped trees; we even bagged ourselves two alligators.

I was getting very attached to our Creole guide's magnificent gumbo — a sort of soupy stew — and we spent a lot of our day catching the freshwater lobsters that he used to add body to the meal. It was during a lazy afternoon of cray fishing that the smell hit us.

The stench came in on the air and I knew immediately that our true quarry was close at hand. I alerted Kent and our guide and we tooled up and went in search of our prey. I knew Kent had found it when I heard him vomiting. I had warned my good friend to wear a mask like mine that covered the mouth nose and eyes, but he had merely tied a bandanna around his lower face, in the manner of a cowboy or bandito.

I turned towards my friend and was greeted by a sight that, even through the tinted glass of my goggles, chilled my heart.

The Vampire stood just less than six feet tall and was so grossly bloated it was almost unrecognizable as having a human shape. Its eyes were so sunken within the swollen purple flesh that it

was blind, and its rank odour meant that it was unable to smell our own.

However, its hearing was still keen, and it opened its blackened maw, showing the merest stumps of teeth, as it thundered suddenly towards the doubled-over form of my batman. Its forward charge took it past where I stood, and with a sharpened stake I struck it once in its rolling, extended belly, and then again in its liquid rear.

The effects were instant — it stopped dead in a howl of pain and blood erupted from its wounds and mouth. The force of the blood from the gushing back wound caught me full in the chest and knocked me to the ground; I was momentarily lost beneath the swamp water and voided offal. I surfaced and the eyes of my prey were upon me – it knew that I was the one who had robbed it of its precious store of blood, its life source, and it was full of rage.

As the blood drained away from its body, the female form beneath emerged from what had been the bloated swamp creature. Marsh weed clung to its body like a mockery of the clothes it no longer wore. I saw the intelligence in the eyes as it took a more defensive stance. Already it was aware that its fate was to be decided here. I threw out my hand and launched something towards it in a slow graceful arc.

I was not mistaken at the intelligence in its face, for it intercepted my gift easily and looked down scornfully at the ash-hewn stake in its grasp. It looked at me and smiled with a mouth red as fresh meat, grasped the stake tight and leapt. I have seen tigers leap with less power and grace than this Vampire achieved from the base of soft swamp mud. It was intent on finishing me off with the very stake I had earlier used to deprive it of its bloody corpulence.

I ducked beneath its lunge, throwing myself again into the swamp water, but it had already turned and was upon me. I felt the point of my own stake pierce my side, but, as I suspected, my denser body, and to some degree my heavy woollen clothing, prevented it from sinking deeply into my flesh.

It was the gamble I needed – I threw the beast over my shoulders and onto the solid earth, pinning it to the ground. It struggled for a moment, and then I watched as it dawned upon the creature that I would have to release it in order to do it any harm – we were in a deadlock.

Now, however, it was my time to smile. I nodded to a point just out of its vision and, as it turned its haemorrhaging eyes towards it, the Vampire saw its advantage was lost. It was looking down the barrel of Kent's revolver.

We removed the lifeless head (you can never be too sure) and left the rest for the gators and crayfish. All part of the natural life cycle of the bayous.

Yeti

I have come across wild men all around the globe and every culture has a different name for them, giving rise to the belief they are all unique. From my experience, however, the wild man is virtually the same the world over, the only difference being the ones you would always note among different castes of humans. Personally, I like the name Yeti; it just feels right.

Description

This huge ape-like humanoid is covered in thick matted fur, generally brown in colour, although variations occur, most notably the blue-white fur in Tibet.

The beast has a domed head, similar to the mountain gorilla, and the similarities do not stop there. The creature also has a hairless face with a heavy-set brow and sloping forehead. Its eyes are deep in colour and very human in appearance. The nose is broad and flat but hooded like ours rather than flared like the gorilla's. The mouth is wide and thin-lipped, the teeth are wide and the mouth has heavy canine fangs top and bottom.

The chin is evident and juts forward, often giving a snaggle-toothed appearance. The ears are tiny versions of our own and sit on the side of the head but higher up. Its shoulders are broad and sloping and end in powerful arms, more defined towards the forearm than the bicep. The hands are leathery, with long fingers, but also resembling our own in that they have an opposable thumb.

The chest is powerful and rises and falls dramatically, suggesting the large and powerful lungs beneath. It tapers to a muscled lower torso and finally rests on powerful legs and large splayed feet.

The Yeti is principally a carnivore, but does have slight omnivore tendencies so that in times of scarcity it will eat roots and berries. Normally however the diet is solely raw meat and fish.

The Yeti is an adept hunter and will happily hunt Man as well as other sources of meat.

Chiefly cave dwellers, they live in small family groups, wholly dependent on the available food supply. They show no signs of civilization, however, in any form — whether clothing, tools or art.

Anthropologists with whom I have shared information tend to believe that we are not necessarily the only branch at the end of the human tree; it is just possible that others may have developed favouring the now-defunct traits of the Neanderthal.

Bodies adapted for chillier climes (as experienced around the Ice Age) would need larger lungs and broader noses to avoid air freezing within the body.

The Yeti has an interesting form of attack — it ambushes. The beast will hide in bushes or climb trees. This is not merely opportunistic behaviour, however, but shows some kind of intelligence, for the Yeti will track its prey and then scout ahead along the most probable path to lay its ambush. When they attack it is with powerful blows of the fists, targeting vulnerable parts and wearing the prey quickly down.

Habitat

Generally remote areas with abundant wildlife and cave systems. Climate does not seem to be a factor as long as the other criteria are met.

The cave systems tend to run deep and often are maze-like in appearance though never tight, as if a long and steady period of coming and going has kept the walkways free of the usual calcification of subterranean cave systems.

Yeti

FIG # 1

FIG #2

FIG #3

FIG #4

Fig #1 Head detail
Fig #2 Attacking stance
Fig #3 Upright walking
Fig #4 Track

Threat

Apart from the hunting and eating of humans, the Yeti is but a small threat compared to, say, the Vampire or Lycanthrope. The real fear comes from the continued existence of a threat to Man's supremacy. If some of our most esteemed explorers are right, there may indeed be whole civilizations deep in the Earth, perhaps like those discovered in the so-called Lindenbrock caverns.

Hunting

The best thing about hunting Yeti is you have the technological advantage. The difficulty is actually finding the Yeti in the first place.

With this in mind, it becomes obvious you need a good guide to the area, preferably one who believes in the Yeti or has seen the beasts themselves. Often the sightings or believers are ridiculed and good guides therefore are almost as difficult to find as the Yetis themselves.

Once you prove you are also a believer, you will hear enough stories to actually map a viable area for hunting. Be aware that the Yeti is often revered by a native population or even seen as sacred; therefore some information may be designed to lead you astray.

Once you know in which area you should look, you will need to do some careful mapping and investigation. During this time it is important not to hunt, but to get a feel of the lay of the land. If Yetis are nearby, you will be watched and after a week or so they will get ready to hunt you.

Yetis are big beasts and therefore when they stalk you it will be obvious that something is on your trail, as long as you are paying attention. They also have a pungent smell, so try to make your journey away from the wind; this will keep you aware of their presence.

The moment the noisy stalking and smell stops, your Yeti has rushed ahead to carry out its ambush. At this stage, stop moving, and take stock of your journey ahead. Ideally, you should take a less obvious route that still keeps the main route within sight. If this is not possible, you need to take heed of any place that might provide as ambush points, particularly trees or overhanging rocks.

You also need to be fully armed. Have to hand a heavy-bladed knife, but also an accurate rifle or powerful handgun. You are now upwind from the Yeti, so smell is not a good guide, and the creature will generally remain quiet right up until the moment of the ambush.

The moment the smell disappears from behind me, I like to

reach straight for my opera glasses (it is the best use I have found for them). These enable me to watch the Yeti take up position and then all I need to do is to find a good vantage point and take aim. Two well-placed shots normally do the trick.

If you don't find the ambush point, then caution is the name of the game. If the Yeti does get to spring its ambush, then you need to act fast. Fire as many shots as possible — the noise alone will throw the beast off its attack and any that hit will do harm. Then drop your gun, a move that I would normally warn against, but since Yeti do not — cannot — use tools they will not pick it up. Instead, pull your knife, move in close and start stabbing.

The Yeti can only get good blows in if it gets a good swing, so keep things intimate. They will growl and bear fangs but as far as I am aware no one alive has ever been bitten. Keep your stabs to the lower abdomen as the blade will enter vital organs. Stabs to the chest will be unlikely to penetrate the muscle or even the ribs. The Yetis have an extra rib (I suppose they didn't give one up to God)

TIPS

Get to know the legends of the area and build up a hunting ground.

Always take an experienced and sympathetic guide.

Try to hunt in pairs — one experienced marksman and one close-combat fighter and tracker.

Optical equipment, such as opera glasses or a telescope, is important — viewing ahead is paramount.

Good maps of the area must be obtained long before you even start your hunt or made during your exploration of the region.

Never start to examine cave systems they are far too easy to be lost in and are more likely to lead to larger groups of Yetis.

---

and the bones are denser. If you get into a tussle in this way, you need to keep your breathing regular — stamina is a must in a scrap like this.

Personal Account

I have been very lucky with some of the people I have had the pleasure to work with on my travels. Brian Houghton Hodgson was a true gentleman, with a real knowledge of the wildlife of Tibet; he was also a loyal subject of the Queen and a seasoned observer of Yeti activity.

Mr. Hodgson, however, wasn't as happy as he could have been

about the hunt and insisted that we should go into the mountains alone. He did not take any weapons of his own, so I felt that a lot rested on my shoulders, but I fully trusted he would be as helpful as he could be.

As an ecologist, he may not have liked the idea of killing a Yeti but he was also a staunch royalist and patriot. I learnt a lot from that man over the month we travelled together and of all the men I have studied with through my life he will always be one of the greats to me.

We had reached the low hills of Tibet and found a cold yet snow-less plateau where we quickly set up a camp, one that was resplendent with all the extravagant equipment necessary to gentlemen of refinement. Once settled, we bade goodbye to our Sherpas and arranged for their return in a fortnight.

We spent our subsequent days moving amongst the hills and taking samples of the region's astonishing and beautiful flora. Three days in I picked up the smell. I pointed it out to Mr. Hodgson and he agreed it was not the warm smell of a bear but the more pungent smell of a primate.

We camped that night, only too aware of the smell on the breeze. My companion rested well but I just kept listening to the night, which was well lit by a full moon. Eventually the sounds of distant snoring came to my ears. I would have chuckled at how unstealthy the Yeti truly was. I took the moment to grab my rifle and hunting knife and moved quietly towards the rock overhang where the snoring was coming from.

It was too high to see for a shot so I climbed up higher. With my knife in my teeth, and my rifle on my back, I broached the overhang and was immediately assaulted by the smell of sweat and rank fur. I crept forward to the sleeping beast and ran my sharp knife across its throat – it didn't even wake – just burbled and died.

I heard a noise on the detritus beneath the overhang and, assuming that Mr. Hodgson had woken and followed me, I leaned over to tell him of my kill. Suddenly I was grabbed by a big gnarled hand that threw me from the ledge. As I struck the rocks, all wind left my body and another Yeti was upon me. I am unsure if it was older or whether its hair was taking on its winter camouflage but it was peppered with tufts of blue-white fur.

It is unusual for Yetis to hunt in pairs, but it seemed in this case that I had stumbled across an older male teaching an adolescent. The younger was dead and the elder was maddened with rage and perhaps with grief. I can only assume what reaction the family group would have on the mentor's companion-less return.

I could see the hate in his eyes and felt the pain caused by my own gun as it dug deep into my back. His fists were raised high above his head before they came slamming down on my chest, and I felt my ribs pop. He raised his fists again and I grabbed a rock beside me and brought it as hard as I could into his genitals. Its broken edge opened the main artery, located near the groin, and I was drenched in a spray of warm sticky blood (not very Marquess of Queensbury of me, I admit). The beast howled and I pulled myself up to my feet, shards of pain moving through my chest.

With some effort I brought the rock in an arch and into the beast's temple. It stumbled around as I unslung my rifle. The barrel was bent so, instead of trying to fire it, I gripped it hard in my hands, and as the Yeti turned to face me again I swung the heavy wooden butt at its head. The blow spun it clean off its feet and I felt a sudden sharpness in my chest. I fell to my knees, dropping the broken rifle. The Yeti was prone, blood besmirching its face, but its chest still rose and fell. I passed out.

I came out of my fever to find myself being cared for by Mr. Hodgson. He had found me two days ago on a cold morning surrounded by blood that wasn't my own. There were no bodies.

To my mind I must have hurt the adult enough for him to flee for cover, taking his dead protégé with him. perhaps to die himself. I had two broken ribs, and one had actually punctured my chest wall causing me great pain and making me black out. It was at a local monastery that I was nursed back to health, whereafter I returned gratefully to England.